DOPPEL-GANGER

A Later-in-Life Romance

By Danielle Bannister

a.k.a. Dani Bannister

This novel is a work of fiction. Names, characters, places and incidents are the product of the author's imagination or are used fictitiously. Any resemblance to actual events, locales, or persons, living or dead, is coincidental.

DANIELLE BANNISTER Dani BANNISTER

Doppelganger
ISBN-13:978-1542365420
ISBN-10: 1542365422
Cover Design by Q Design
Edited by Kathy Lapeyre

Dedication

I dedicate this book to my dear friend and author, Julie Cassar, who gave me the idea for this story via a text message while I was standing in line at the grocery store, bemoaning to her the fact that I didn't know what to write about for my next book. She told me to write about a woman standing in line at a grocery store. So, I did. Naturally, I had to name the main character after her in thanks.

Chapter 1

I was not having a mid-life crisis no matter what my friends might have said when they found out I'd left. The decision to pack up and leave everything behind wasn't irrational. It was going to be the most logical thing I had ever done, in theory.

Everyone has a breaking point, and I had reached mine. Enough was enough. I was done. Done with the commute…done with the smog…done with the crowds. Done with fake people and the even faker tits that basked in the LA sun and I was most definitely done with my former boyfriend, Anthony, and his perfect wife getting pregnant with kid number three.

There it was; the straw that broke the camel's back.

So, I left. It felt good, too. For once in my life, I was taking charge of my own destiny. At least, that's what I kept telling my mother's voice each time she popped into my head during the twenty-three hour drive across the country.

Julie, honey, what are you running from?

Really bad choices, Ma.

When are you going to settle down and make me some grandbabies?

Um, never.

Maybe you could go back to school and finish your degree this time? It's so hard to explain to people what it is you do.

Tell them I work in an office. I'm a temp. It's not that hard.

Why don't you move back home? I heard Daniel Howards got divorced.

Thanks, Ma, I'll pass.

Those are the types of questions my mother would ask if I called—which is precisely why I didn't when I left. I chose to avoid the lectures and reminders that I had failed in life, yet again. I just wanted out.

My mother, of course, had no idea about my affair with Anthony. If she had discovered that I was the *other woman* she would have gotten down on bended knee and prayed for my soul, even though she hadn't been to church in years. The fact that her daughter had been sleeping around with a married man for the last three years, however, might be enough to send her back.

I'd send her a text whenever I landed someplace. When it was too late for her to talk me out of it.

The plan had been to end in Maine, the literal farthest away I could get from LA, but I ended up pulling over somewhere in New Hampshire to ask directions from a woman who was putting up a For Rent sign in her yard. We started chatting, and I decided, on the spot, I needed to live in *that* house.

New Hampshire was just as a good a state as any, as far as I was concerned. Now all that was left to do was unpack. Not that I'd brought much. Only as much stuff that fit in the rented SUV. The rest, I'd left behind, along with a note to my landlord letting him know not to expect a renewal of my lease. But before I began unloading the car to officially start my new life, I needed wine. And maybe some Doritos. Okay, and some ice cream too.

Thanks to the GPS in the SUV, I found the center of town…if you could call it that, and I pulled into the lot of the most Mayberry-looking grocery store anyone could possibly imagine.

"It's gotta have wine…even Andy Griffith needed to get drunk now and then."

I found my way inside and winced at the slight jingle noise the door made as I entered.

"Wow." That was the only word I could come up with for a store as tiny as this. It had five aisles total and not one dedicated for booze. This might be a problem. It was a far cry from the Big Saver stores I was accustomed to.

I grabbed one of the few carts by the door and started the hunt. Mercifully, the end of the first aisle had a small selection of alcoholic choices. I grabbed the biggest bottle of red wine they had and placed it into my cart where it rolled around precariously, as though drunk on its own existence.

One essential down. The chips proved to be a bit harder to find. I frowned. Nothing was where it should be. *Why were food stores all so different?* Couldn't they have a meeting or something and all agree on the same basic layout? No, instead, I had to waste my barely viable years searching for panty liners, olives, and makeup to cover up the zit growing on my forehead. Apparently, that defined life in your forties: leakage, sodium cravings, and acne. Honestly, when was the zit thing going to end? Sure, I'd been under a lot of stress lately, but was it really necessary to give me a third eye too?

Annoyed, I shoved the cart forward and began rolling my shoulders in small circles to ease some of the tension lodged there from the long hours behind the wheel. I'd never driven so long in such a short time and had no intention of doing it again. Not that I could, even if I wanted to. My funds were all but dried up.

I had saved some money by sleeping in my car at night instead of staying in a hotel, leaving me with about two hundred bucks to my name. I tried not to feel guilty about putting in a second bag of chips. I'd earned those.

As I rounded the corner in search of ice cream, I almost crashed, head on, into another cart. My wine rolled to the end of its metal cage and gave off a cringe-worthy *thunk* but, thankfully, remained intact.

"Oh, I'm sorry," the lady pushing the offending cart said. I glared at her for almost murdering my wine while I sized her up. She was about my age, maybe a few years younger, with a pudgy toddler in the front of her cart grabbing at everything within his sticky grasp. I tried not to gag at the crusty boogers lining the edge of his nose. I shivered. Kids were so gross.

"It's okay," I mumbled, trying to weave my cart around her.

The woman's smile abruptly faded. Likely because she realized I was an *out-of-towner*. Her eyes grew wide, and she took a step back. She gaped at me as though trying to form a sentence. Engaging in small talk with the locals was not high on my agenda, so I whipped around to the next aisle and came face to face with a line of purple and green plastic packages. *Oh, pads. Excellent.* One step closer to leaving this joint and drowning myself in wine.

When I placed the liners in my cart, I couldn't shake the feeling I was being watched, so I turned to glance behind me and saw the same woman sneaking a peek at me through an endcap of beef jerky before she dashed away.

"Okay…" Clearly, these small town folks didn't like strangers in their midst.

Opting to pass up the hunt for mint chocolate chip ice cream just to get the hell out of Dodge, I made my way toward the sole checkout person. Sole. As in…they only had one register. Not just one lane open. One lane total. Maybe moving to New Hampshire wasn't such a good idea.

I let out a breath and got in line behind a man in his seventies getting a shit-ton of cat food. Each can rang up *by hand.*

Oh. My. God. *I'm going to die waiting for this man to get his month's supply of cat food.*

Then again, maybe this was what life in a small town would teach me: to slow down, smell the roses and all that jazz. I mean, it wasn't as if I were late for anything. I had no job, and no one was waiting for me back at the rental. So why lose my cool over the change of pace? *Embrace it, Jules. The wine will still taste as sweet an hour from now.*

The towers of tuna slowly disseminated, exposing a sliver of the black conveyor belt, so I started to put my own items down.

"Looks like Hansel and Gretel prefer the flaked salmon," the woman at the register was saying as she plucked at the keys.

"Oh, they love it, Penny," the man said. "Hansel will try and get Gretel's before she's even done. I have to separate them when they eat."

The woman nodded sagely. "I have to do that with my three too," she said, bagging the cans in one of the cloth bags he had brought. "Oh, and you got one of those Lean Cuisines. You on a diet, Frank?"

My eyes widened in horror. Was this woman going to talk to me about my purchases as well? Would she seriously ask me if my panty liners really *were* super absorbent? Or if that liter and a half bottle of wine was just for me? Doesn't she know the Cashier Code? *Ask the customers if they found everything and how they want their items bagged. That's it. Take their money and move on. Do not engage. Do. Not. Engage.*

I began to panic about what I was going to say to her when I noticed the old man handed her a few bills. Actual paper money. Did this joint even have a credit card machine? I looked around and didn't see any signs of one. *Oh, hell.* I was screwed.

Digging into my purse, I fished around in my wallet and, luckily, found a few twenties I had shoved in there before I left LA. The cash was all I had left from the sale of my *promise* ring; the one Anthony had given me. The ring that meant absolutely nothing in the end.

The cashier said her goodbyes to the cat man before she looked up at me with that same stranger-danger stare the lady with the snotty-nosed kid had given me.

"Do I know you?" she asked, slowly taking my liners and pulling them closer to the register.

"I highly doubt it," I said, reaching into my purse, this time to find my sunglasses.

She continued to bag the groceries with a watchful eye.

"Not from around these parts?"

"Nope."

"It's a little early for the foliage to bloom. Most tourists come by next month."

"Foliage? I could care less about leaf color," I said.

She nodded slowly. "So, just passing through, then?" she fished.

"Look, can I just pay for my food and go?"

She gawked up at me, clearly offended, but sped up, nonetheless.

"You got an ID for the wine?" Her cheery tone had left.

I lowered my glasses and blinked at her. "I'm forty-two."

She pursed her lips. "And as soon as you show me that ID, you can have the wine."

So much for small town charm. I sighed and dug back into my purse for my ID but couldn't find it.

"Shit. It must have fallen out it in the car."

"Mmhmm," she said, sliding the wine aside, away from my bags. *This chick was actually confiscating my wine!*

Behind me, sticky-kid-lady started to unload her items. She and the cashier exchanged a few glances, probably making fun of me in their small town hick code way. I turned to glare at the mom. I saw her pointing at something behind me. She froze when she caught me looking at her.

"What?" I asked them. Neither woman said anything, but the cashier bagged the bottle of wine.

"No charge, dear. You have yourself a good day. New Hampshire welcomes you back." She smiled at me.

Confused, I snatched the bags and started to leave the store, pausing only when I spotted the object of their attention. It was nothing more than a large display of cheesy tabloids. I frowned and was about to turn away when I noticed something.

"What the hell?" I whispered, yanking my sunglasses off.

On the cover of every single magazine was a picture of a woman who looked *exactly* like me.

Chapter 2

Confusion swept over me as I made it back to the SUV. Something didn't make sense. The name associated with the pictures was not mine but that of a mega movie star, Morgan Malone. Now, I may not be a movie buff, but I just watched two movies she was in: *Chase the Night* and *The Butcher Says Die* within the last few months, and she most certainly did not look like me in those films. Sure, we were both blonde and tall and maybe had a similar heart-shaped face, but that was where the similarities ended. She was a full five years younger than me and actually cared about what her body looked like, whereas I had paid little attention to the rolls of chub forming around my midsection since hitting my forties.

So what the hell was going on? I dug out my phone and did a search on her name and clicked the first link that popped up: *Morgan Malone Barely Recognizable After Corrective Surgery.*

"Corrective Surgery?" I said, "*Sure* it was." My eyes skimmed over the article…desperate for answers.

Film icon, Morgan Malone, arrived on the red carpet last Friday night to help promote boyfriend, Kade Dermont's, new sci-fi thriller, *Three if by Sky.* The film star was virtually unrecognizable after having corrective surgery to fix a deviated septum. Onlookers gasped at her new look wondering why nose surgery would alter the rest of her appearance quite so drastically. One star at the event, who wished to remain anonymous, said, "Apparently her chin and eyes were deviated as well."

When asked for a reply to these allegations, Morgan simply stated, "No comment."

After her public appearance, however, Morgan has been absent from all her social media accounts and our eye in the sky choppers indicate her limo left her LA estate Saturday morning. It is rumored that she has retreated to one of her many mansions to wait out the media backlash of her shocking new appearance. Her manager, Cassandra Evans, issued a statement Saturday morning indicating Morgan was "taking some time off to prepare for an upcoming project" though our reports found no evidence of any current film productions starring Ms. Malone. Which leaves some to wonder if the surgery was merely a botched attempt to hang onto her fading youth and fame.

There is even speculation after this most recent outing that she won't appear at her own premiere later this month.

Click on our gallery of before and after pics and let us know what you think of her new look? Gorgeous? Or Gruesome?

I sat in the SUV for several minutes just re-reading the article before, like an idiot, I read the vile-filled thread of insulting comments that followed:

"She looks like my Uncle Steve!"

"Hideous! Why can't celebs leave their faces alone? So gross!"

"She needs surgery to fix her surgery."

"I'd paper bag her."

I read for several minutes. Each comment was more of the same. Hateful words that were, essentially, bashing *my* appearance.

"Well, this calls for a glass of wine. Or ten," I muttered.

I started the car and turned on the GPS to find the rental house. My sense of direction was based on being able to see an ocean on one side of me, but out here, I had no landmark to orient my pea-brain to. The roads here in the boondocks twisted and turned in seemingly random ways, which didn't help matters.

While the GPS got me to the house without failure, it couldn't help me find where the wine glasses were packed. That was one item I knew I'd need once I'd settled somewhere, but which random container were they in? I scanned the small living room that held my laundry bins, empty trash cans, and five dresser drawers. Just the drawers, though, the actual bureau wouldn't fit into the SUV. That was fine. I only wanted the clothes in them anyway. Furniture could be replaced. Hell, it all could, but I was trying to be practical with what little funds I had at my disposal, and clothes seemed an immediate necessity sort of thing. Furniture, not so much.

All in all, this move worked out far better than I anticipated. I lucked out finding a furnished rental because I had been planning to sleep on the floor and live out of my dresser drawers until I could get a job and afford an actual mattress. Now, I was living in the lap of luxury…if only I could find where I packed the sheets.

As soon as I sat on the lumpy brown sofa, I knew the search for the wine glasses was officially over. I was too tired to care about formalities. I unscrewed the cap of the wine and drank straight from the bottle. It was cheap as hell, but I knew I would have no hope of finding the wine cork anytime soon, and there was no way I was going to be able to get through this night without, at least half of the bottle.

As I downed the third chug, my cell phone rang. I fumbled around, feeling between the couch cushions where it had apparently been eaten, and I picked it up on the fourth ring.

I recognized the ringtone after the first note. “Hey, Macy,” I said as I pressed the bottle to my forehead, trying to numb a headache that was forming. This call certainly wasn’t going to help get rid of it. I knew what Macy wanted; it was the obligatory BFF check-in call. She was the only person alive who knew I’d left town and why, but I *so* wasn’t in a mood to pretend to be fine.

“Jules!” Macy squealed. I had to hold the phone away from my ear until she was finished. She squeals when she gets excited. Don’t ask why I know this. Let’s just say we were roommates a million years ago, and the walls were, unfortunately, thin. “OMG. Did you see what Morgan Malone did to her face? She looks just like you now!”

I groaned. “Yeah, I was sort of hoping I was the only one who noticed that.”

“For real, Jules, I almost spit out my cappuccino when I saw it. Hella freakish!” I rolled my eyes. I loved Macy, dearly, even though she was a walking contradiction. On the outside, she was organized, career driven, and fiery, but to hear her talk sometimes…you would never have guessed she was an editor at one of the biggest book publishers in the country.

We met in college and even though we went in completely opposite directions career-wise (you know, her having one and me not) we became fast friends. I’ll admit it; I’m a high-maintenance friend. Or, at least, I was. The old Julie was weak—in constant need of comfort for all of my mistakes—pathetic. No more. Things were going to change here. I could feel it.

“It was just too weird, I had to tell you about it,” Macy continued.

“Yeah, I got some strange looks at the grocery store. Morgan’s face was in all the papers. It was creepy.”

“How cool is that, though? You have a famous doppelganger!” I could hear her bouncing up and down at the idea.

“Oh, yeah, I’m thrilled, just what I an introvert wants—to be mistaken for a famous person.”

"Please, are you kidding?" she said. "I would be all over that in a heartbeat. I'd sign people's autographs, get into places for free. Girl, you could work that."

I took another drink. "Yeah, sounds like loads of fun."

Her excitement level dropped, so I knew things were about to get serious. I took another drink.

"So, how is it in the other half of the world? Are you in Maine yet? Is it as bad as I think? Is it all vanilla up there?"

I laughed, despite the throb in my temples. "I didn't make it to Maine, but I got close enough. Let's just say if you came for a visit, though, you'd be easy to point out in a crowd."

She gagged. "Seriously?"

I cocked my head, trying to think. "It's pretty pasty here."

"Well, you'll fit right in then," she sassed.

It was true. My naturally translucent skin, a tone that made me stand out like a freak in LA, actually blended perfectly into the fold here, which was exactly what I wanted…to disappear.

"How you holding up?" Macy asked, prompting a sigh from me. I knew what she was really asking: did I regret coming out here? Had I made a huge mistake? Had I gone off the deep end instead of thinking this through? The truth was, I wasn't totally sure of what my answer was going to be.

"I'm good. Great. I'm almost finished unpacking," I lied.

"Oh, send me pictures! I wanna see your place."

"Um," I looked around at the mess. "I will when it's all done."

"Fine." I could see her pouting, even over the phone. She got a lot of things she wanted with that pout.

Not to be put off the scent, she kept fishing. "So where did you end up? Anywhere you think you could work?" I could hear the skepticism in her voice. She was trying to be supportive of her friend who was clearly having a midlife crisis, all while hiding the air of *I told you this was a bad idea* tone.

"I honestly don't know where the hell I am, truth be told. Some tiny ass town in New Hampshire. I'll let you know when I do. As for places to work, I saw some Help Wanted signs when I went into town, so I'll scope those out tomorrow." The lies just kept flowing. It was surprisingly easy when there was no one around to contradict them.

"Great. That's great," Macy said. An uncomfortable pause filled the space where neither of us knew what to say. "I miss you." I heard her sniff softly.

Despite trying to hold it together, I teared up too. There was an unwritten code among best friends: No one cries alone.

"I miss you too, chicky, but I had to do this. I had to, for my own sanity. I just—couldn't be around Anthony anymore, you know?"

"I know, but did you have to move so far away? Couldn't you have just gone to Oregon or something? I mean, as it is, I'd have to take time off and book a flight just to spend time with you."

She couldn't conceal the hurt in her question, the disappointment.

I let out a breath. "That's exactly why I had to move across the country. I had to remove all possibility of Anthony deciding to show up on my door for a quickie, or worse, have him try to convince me to come back." Secretly, though, that was my hope. That he'd realize I was gone and find me…fight for me. Put me as his top priority, but that was just another lie I told myself. He didn't care enough about me to do that. He'd forget about me long before I forgot about him.

I paused and took another drink. The buzz was beginning to drown out the throbbing. "It was a toxic relationship, Macy. You know that," I said as much for her benefit as mine. "You've been telling me the same thing from day one. I needed to stop being his backup plan. I needed to matter, you know?"

"You mattered to me," Macy said in a weak, barely audible voice.

I smiled through the tears that had formed. "I know, but as long as I stayed on the west coast, I was always going to be just his mistress, the toy he got to play with when he got bored at home."

Thinking about it made me swallow down my own revulsion. I hated that I had allowed myself to become that. The fact that I'd allowed it for three years straight was downright pathetic.

"I know, girl." Macy sighed. "I just hate it."

"Well, if it's any comfort, bumpkin life is pretty hellish, so far."

With that, the conversation shifted easily into the observations I'd made here among the plaid-loving locals. It was hard to suppress the absolute beauty of the neighborhood, though. People out in LA rarely got to see so much green. It seemed a little too perfect to be real, if I were being honest. And the traffic! Absolutely *no* traffic here. I couldn't get over it.

I started to unpack as we talked. Macy was going off about the skanks she saw walking around with her ex and then merged effortlessly to the book deal she had snatched out from another agent. I let her talk. It was good just to hear her voice. Her laugh was infectious, and soon I found myself chuckling right along with her. She really was a hoot. I'd miss that the most about Macy, her vibrant energy. Even though I knew our connection was strong, our relationship would fade soon enough. The distance between us would finally break the bond we had created during the last nineteen years. No amount of social media or phone calls could ever hope to replace a pub crawl, a shoe-shopping spree or even the gentle squeeze of a hug you didn't know you needed.

I understood that reality before moving across country, and I still came. It was one of the sacrifices I knew I'd need to make in order to figure out who I was. Life was about choices. It was high time I started making some good ones.

I hung up with Macy and decided it was time to make another good decision: deleting Anthony's number off my phone.

Pulling up his info, my finger hovered over the trash can icon that would finally remove him from my life. One simple press of my finger and he'd be out of my life for good.

So why the hell couldn't I push that button?

I glanced down at the bottle of wine. "It's the booze, Jules. You'll do it tomorrow when your head is clear."

Taking another swig, I repeated my mantra. "Tomorrow. Your new life starts tomorrow."

Chapter 3

I hate my bladder. I curse its name every morning at 5:33 when it decides to wake me up. It doesn't matter what time I go to bed, it always wakes me up at 5:33 or thereabouts. There's no point trying to go back to sleep after, either. By the time I'm done, the brain has flipped on and any attempt to get more shut-eye will inevitably be thwarted by pesky thoughts. Thoughts I'd rather not have at the moment. No time for idle minds today.

Stumbling over the heaps of my crap, still unpacked, I found my way to the coffee maker. That was the one thing I made sure to bring. In fact, it rode shotgun, tucked safely inside a laundry bin full of essentials. No coffee, no workee.

While the brain juice percolated, I dug around for something to eat. I know I packed a box of protein bars somewhere.

I turned on a light as the sun had yet to quite touch the sky, making the outside a deep peacock blue. It's the sort of sky my mom would call *a transitional sky*. She swore when she saw a sky that color a major change was about to happen in her life. I wondered if she might have been right.

Looking around at the mess that was the current state of my own, I sighed. The unpacking fairy hadn't come again. *Dammit.*

"I suppose I should tackle the rest of this shit, huh?" I asked the couch, my only real friend since I'd moved in.

Pulling my hair up into a ponytail with the elastic band from around my wrist, I rolled up the sleeves on my hoodie and picked a random box.

I should have taken two seconds before I left to think logically about what to pack in which container, but since I'd snapped, logical thinking wasn't part of the mix. I was packed and gone in a matter of minutes. I think part of me thought I would stop a few hours into the trip, shake out of my insanity, and turn back.

But I didn't. With each mile I'd driven, the stronger my resolve had became. It was weird…almost as though the universe was letting me know I was on the right path. I wasn't the type to believe in signs or fate, but this seemed right somehow. Extremely out of my comfort zone, but *right* nonetheless.

I approached piles of random crap heaped on the couch as the last drips were entering the coffee pot. That's when I heard the squeal of tires outside.

No one in LA would have even noticed the sound, but out here, where the landscape was so damn quiet, I had to check out the window to see what was going on.

I rushed over and pulled back the curtain to peer outside. There, directly in front of my driveway sat an old beat-up truck. The engine was still on, and its headlights beamed brightly into the pre-dawn sky. I heard a shriek of fear from what looked like a guy from the passenger's seat, and then a second man got out and rushed to the front of the truck. He had paused for a moment before checking under it.

"Please say you didn't just run over a skunk," I muttered.

As though hearing me, the guy's head popped up, and he saw me peeking out of the curtain. He waved.

"Shit," I said, instantly trying to hide behind the wall. He'd seen me.

Go away. Go away. Go away.

The knock on my door a few seconds later confirmed an introvert's worst nightmare. I was going to have to talk to him: a perfect stranger, and I wasn't even wearing a bra. At least my zit had gone down overnight. Otherwise, I may not have opened the door.

Cursing under my breath, I reached for the door, wishing it had the same chain-lock mechanism as my old apartment. Did they not have serial killers in New Hampshire?

Opening it a crack, I peered out. "Yes?" I asked, keeping my foot on the back of the door, ready to slam it shut if he pulled anything funny.

The man stood a few inches away. He had some five o'clock shadow going on that was greying in a few spots. His face was kind and cute. Figures. I had an attractive guy at my door, and I was in pajamas with no makeup on and reeking of morning breath.

"Hi. My name is Scott Jacobs." I paused, waiting for a reason his was supposed to matter to me, other than his voice being really sexy. "Um, do you happen to own an orange tabby cat?" he asked, pulling off his hat and revealing a head of matted down salt and pepper curls. *Damn, he was cute.* Not supermodel hot, but more like a weathered lumberjack hot.

My eyes flicked toward his left hand. No ring…I glanced back up at him when I noticed steel grey eyes staring back at me. *Jesus.* I'd never actually seen someone with that color eyes before. They were a little jarring but not at all unattractive. I actually had to shake my head to clear my mind from the spell those eyes seemed to put me under.

"Come again?" I asked because I completely had forgotten what he'd said.

"Um, the cat? Is it yours?" he asked.

I blinked at him, blushing suddenly at what must have been my overt ogling. He didn't seem upset by that fact, however, because he gave me a sweet grin, one that showed off two perfect dimples. *Well, shit.* I was a sucker for dimples. Dated a lot of bad men just because of those stupid things.

"No, I'm not a cat person," I finally said. His face shifted from the worry a moment ago to straight-up relief.

"Good, 'cause I think I may have killed it."

"Oh." My eyes darted toward the beam of light on the road. "Ew."

He appeared sick with guilt. "Yeah."

"Well, thanks for stopping by," I said while trying to close the door.

"Hey, would you mind taking a look to see if you recognize it? I hate to just leave it there if it belongs to one of your neighbors," he asked. I started to protest when he begged. "Please." The pleading nature in his tone of voice made my pulse speed up. Couple that with those eyes and his dimples and I would have said yes to just about anything.

Whoa. I hadn't even thought of another guy other than Anthony in years, and now here I was having a virtual wet dream with this random guy. I didn't know how to process it all, so I got defensive. Clearly, this jackass was playing a game with me, using his looks like catnip to lure me out of my house.

"You want me to leave the safety of my house, unarmed, and bend over a truck in the dark to check and see if I know the cat you just killed? Look, you may be cute, but I wasn't born yesterday. Go kill the next door neighbor instead," I said, closing the door.

From behind my locked door, I heard him say, "I'm not a murderer."

"Says the man who just killed a cat."

"Hey, it was an accident." He sounded genuinely hurt, not pissed off like a thwarted bad guy might be at a slammed door in the face.

I waited for him to say something else, but all I heard was the reluctant heavy shuffle of his feet walking down my drive…and away from me.

For some reason, I couldn't let that happen, so I opened the door again. "I better not regret this," I whispered to my warm, safe house. I grabbed my cell and turned on the flashlight app and followed the dude outside.

"Hey, wait up."

Scott turned and held the glow of his cell phone in my direction. His smile was so sweet.

"Thanks. I don't know this road well. I never take it, but for some odd reason, we took the long way home," he said, scratching at the back of his head.

"Yeah, well if you kill me, I swear to God I will haunt you till your dying day."

He turned around, and I flashed his face with my light. *I know, I'm a jerk.* He smiled a great smile, though not with completely straight teeth. They were the tiniest bit askew. It was almost as if he had had braces as a child, but they had shifted into the perfect fit for his face.

"Where is this thing?" I said, trying to force my eyes off him. It was too dangerous to linger there for long.

"I think it's under my tire. On the driver's side," he said, walking toward the truck.

Just then, a second voice broke through the morning air. "Oh my God, is this the owner? Ma'am, we are so sorry we killed your cat. It just ran out from nowhere," the passenger in the truck prattled in such a way as to set my *gaydar* off the charts. One look at the clearly flamboyant man in the truck confirmed my suspicion. I checked back at my farmer-man and sighed. *Of course. They were a couple.*

"Pity," I whispered. All the attractive men were always married or gay. Guess that was the same no matter where you lived.

"What's a pity?" the dude with the dimples asked.

I shook my head. "About the animal," I covered.

"Scott, can we just move the thing and go?" the man in the truck wailed. "I have a sixteen-hour shift in no less than six hours, and I need to get some beauty sleep."

"I know, Liam, just give me a minute, okay?" Scott hissed.

As they bickered with each other like an old married couple, I got a closer look at their clothes in the light of the high beams that shot dual spotlights onto the road. It appeared that they both wore green medical scrubs.

Figures. He's a doctor, too.

"If I can find the owner, I want to apologize." Scott looked at me and shrugged. "It's the decent thing to do."

"The decent thing would have been not to hit it in the first place," I snorted.

His eyes narrowed. "You're not from around here, are you?"

"Nope," I said, approaching the front of the truck. "LA girl here. So, I won't have a clue who this cat belongs to." *So why the hell was I out here?*

I bent down and squinted into the darkness with my cell light.

Oh, hell.

Something was there, and it was most definitely not dead. The resounding kitten meow was unmistakable.

Scott knelt down with me to look.

"Christ. You didn't kill it!" I yelled.

"I didn't?"

"No, poor thing looks hurt, though." I reached under the truck, half expecting the kitten to bite me for trying to help it, but instead it purred. This is where most girls would melt and go *awww* and get all girly. Not me. I've never had pets. They don't make my heart melt. I'm not even sure what one does with a pet. As evidence of my ignorance, I held it in my hand, stretched out far from me as if it were from Krypton. "Is its leg supposed to look like that?" I asked, glancing down at a hind leg, dangling significantly lower than the other one.

Scott came closer and gently touched the cat's leg. It cried out in pain. "Oh, man, it's broken."

I blew hair out of my eyes. "Can you fix it? You're a doctor, right?"

"I'm not a doctor," he said, trying to examine the kitten I was holding out in the headlights. "But I can tell you it's a girl." He smirked.

"You're not a doctor, but you're wearing scrubs…are you a medical student?" I pulled the kitten back into my arms.

"No. I'm a nurse." His jaw set firm under his stubble.

A nurse? I could hear Macy's voice in my head. She lived near a hospital. Every time she saw a hot, male nurse, she'd whisper *murse alert*. I'd roll my eyes at her lame made-up word, and yet…that's just what this guy was: a hot male nurse. Well, a hot, gay *murse* who just ran over a kitten. This was my life. I couldn't help but chuckle at the insanity of it all.

"You know, there's no shame in being a nurse just because I'm a guy. I don't find anything laughable about wanting to help people."

I stiffened in defense at being called out for laughing, so naturally, I took it out on him.

"Yeah, well, does that desire to help extend to kittens? Because clearly, she needs a vet. You got one of them in this rinky-dink town?"

"Actually, we do." His voice was firm. I'd upset him.

"Look, I'm sorry. I'm normally not this rude, it's just…it's really freaking early, and I haven't had coffee…"

"It's okay. I'm used to it."

"No. I was wrong to laugh about your job. It's a decent and respectable job. It's a hell of a lot more that what I do, so I'm sorry. Really." I looked into his eyes, searching for forgiveness.

"Well, thank you for that." He seemed to mean it. "I think we'd best get the kitten to Stan's place. He's the vet," he said, looking down at me. Scott reached out for the kitten and placed her gently into the warmth of his hat.

Okay. At that, my heart kind of melted. The bright orange tabby did look awfully damn cute inside his navy blue knit hat.

"Wait, we have to go to the vet now?" Liam grumbled.

"Don't worry, I'll drop you off first. I'm off till Wednesday."

"Pfft. Three days off. You NICU nurses have it easy. You wouldn't last a day in the ER," Liam said, looking down at his nails.

"What does NICU mean?" I asked, curious.

Even though it was still pretty dark out, I swear I saw him blush.

"Neonatal Intensive Care Unit."

I waited for the idiot's definition as I still had no idea what that meant.

"I work in the nursery."

"Oh," I said, surprised.

"My specialty is with really sick infants, premature babies, at-risk mothers and such, but we don't get a lot of those in this neck of the woods, so I care for a lot of healthy babies too. I give them their first medical care, and help moms figure out nursing, that sort of thing."

"Right…" I said, as though I had any understanding of what being a mom entailed.

"Yeah, I know, there's not a lot of guys in the field." He grimaced again but outstretched his non kitten-holding hand. "Well, I guess I should get going. It was nice to meet you—"

"Jules," I offered. "Well, Julie Green, but people call me Jules 'cause I guess that last syllable is too hard to say."

"Nice to meet you, Julie." He smiled uncomfortably and then handed the kitten through the window of the truck for Liam to hold.

"Awww, isn't she adorable?" Liam purred. "Okay, fine, we can go to the vet first."

I smiled. Her little orange-striped head was barely poking out of the hat. They were cute together. Not just the kitten and Liam, but Liam, and Scott too.

"Good luck," I said to the kitten. "To you too," I focused on Scott as he walked back to his truck.

"Thanks for your help," he said, shutting the door.

I nodded. "I'd say anytime, but I don't really want you running over any more kittens."

He laughed. "Hey, sorry to have woken you so early."

"It's okay. I was up anyway. My bladder has a twisted sense of humor."

Why do I say these things out loud?

"Right. Well, I better get going," he said, although he didn't move.

"Watch out for moose. I hear they fight back if you hit them." I turned and didn't look back, even though I wanted to take one last glance at what could have been the perfect guy had he only been straight, but I didn't. I kept moving forward.

No more looking back for me. Never again. Those days were done.

Chapter 4

After a morning like that, I figured I might as well make today the one when I buckled down and started to look for a job. It would mean venturing back into town where those stupid magazines likely were, and where more people might mistake me for a famous chick, but it had to be done. I had nothing left to pay next month's rent. Besides, sooner or later, they'd figure out I was a nobody and leave me alone. Then, I could retreat back into life as a wallflower, and the world could continue to spin on its axis again.

I shivered when I checked the temperature on my cell. Fifty-four degrees. *Brr*. I was tempted to put my bathrobe on over the only two long-sleeved shirts I'd packed but resisted only because of my vanity. I hadn't thought to pack anything even remotely warm.

Another shiver rocked through me as I opened the door. In frustration, I ran my hands over my face. Like it or not, I was going to have to find something warmer to wear, and soon, before I froze my tits off. *I'm told it snows here, and I don't even own a jacket.*

First, I needed a job, and I needed one today.

With a sigh and a rumbling stomach, I headed out into the crisp morning. Behind my large-rimmed sunglasses, I heard the sound of a few fallen leaves as they crushed under my feet. I paused at the SUV and opted to walk into town. I needed to save what little gas was in the tank for when I returned the damn thing later today. How I was getting home from the rental office, I had no idea. I'd worry about that problem after I got back, hopefully with a job.

With teeth chattering, I walked on the wrong side of the road to get the benefit of the sun's warmth. From the hill where my house was perched, I began walking down the *sometimes there, sometimes not* sidewalk. I couldn't figure out any rhyme or reason for the pavement disappearing. It was as though only some patches of this hill had been designed for pedestrians. Did the city planners just decide that no one actually walked the full length of the road?

After a few minutes of nothing but trees, I spotted a tiny cluster of buildings I assumed was the town. At almost nine o'clock, there were literally only a handful of cars on the road. *Don't people here have to work, or is everyone on permanent vacation?*

Once I got into town, I found Main Street easy enough. It appeared as a quaint, cheesy town on some bed and breakfast brochure or online tourist site. Little mom and pop shops were sandwiched in a row of small brick buildings on either side of the one-way street. Some businesses had big bowls of water out for their four-legged friends while others displayed massive potted plants by their entryways that gobbled up much of the already narrow cobbled sidewalk.

There was no trash on the street, like none…and I hadn't seen a single homeless guy yet. I half-wondered if I'd mistakenly walked onto a movie set because it was just too perfect looking. I actually checked around for a camera crew, convinced I was about to spoil a hot set, but I couldn't see any signs of one, so I proceeded down the street in search of a Help Wanted sign.

A sudden whiff of coffee hit my nose as I approached one corner of the intersection, causing my stomach to go off again. A coffee shop sporting the name of Must Love Coffee winked seductively at me. *Hey, I love coffee.* It was a sign. I needed more coffee to get me through this day. My fingers were freezing, too, so I opted to eat. A noisy stomach probably wouldn't make a good first impression on a job search, after all.

The coffee shop was quaint in its attempt to look retro. It had dark walls and a large fireplace with large leather chairs and a few old signs from the fifties and sixties all boasting the benefits of coffee. The rest of the place had typical small circular tables anyone might find even in the coffee shops in LA. Only the glaringly white employees and lack of a massive line revealed the fact that I was still in the boonies.

As I waited for the two elderly people in front of me to order, I noticed several of the tables were filled. All the ladies were wearing dresses, and the men sported ties. I glanced down at my skinny jeans and platform sandals. Adding warm shoes to my ever growing list of things that I didn't have was a must. Biting my lip, I felt remarkably underdressed for a coffee shop, which was weird. Why was everyone so dressed up?

The line moved forward and an older woman, maybe in her late sixties, approached and asked for my order.

I glanced up at the large black chalkboard above her that boasted their selection.

"Wow," I said, aloud in response to the prices.

"Wow, what?" a voice said from behind me. I looked back. There was Scott, standing right behind me.

Wow, those eyes are even more stunning in the sunlight.

I stood there, staring at him for a few seconds, suddenly unable to form a coherent thought.

"Um, wow, the prices here are really cheap," I finally said.

He nodded. The hat from this morning was gone. In its place was freshly washed hair, though the curls didn't seem to want to be contained by the wet hair. The stubble he had sported earlier was gone, which was a pity, but it highlighted those damn dimples. Deep lines shot out like fireworks from the corners of his eyes, showcasing a life full of laughter. I'd always found those lines wildly attractive.

My eyes flitted away from his and noticed he had on a tan V-neck sweater and a tie. Another stupid tie.

"Why is everyone in this town so dressed up? Somebody die?"

Scott laughed, bringing out those wonderful wrinkles. "It's Sunday. A lot of folks dress up for church."

"Ah. Church. Right."

I quickly placed my order for a latte, after which I was given a number and told someone would bring it to me.

Placing the number on a nearby table, I looked back at Scott. “I guess I sort of lost track of what day it is, although, if I’m being honest, I’m not much of a church girl,” I said as a last ditch effort not to sound like a complete asshole for not knowing it was Sunday.

“You don’t say?” He grinned.

“Yeah, that whole bleeding Jesus on a cross thing reminding me of my sins never really worked for me,” I said, shivering against the image of it. My mom had forced me to attend church when I was younger, but I had stopped going in fourth grade. She had insisted I be baptized as a child. Insisted, that my soul had to be saved…just in case.

I grabbed the first empty chair I could find and sat, waiting impatiently for my coffee. I was too flustered to order anything to eat, which meant I’d have to go back after Scott left. That boy made my head mushy.

“Church carries a lot of baggage for some people,” I heard Scott say as he slid into a chair at the table beside me. He placed his numbered card beside mine. “Is it okay if I sit here?”

His voice was deep, yet silky, like butter. He’d be a great radio announcer or public speaker. From the lines of his sweater, I noticed his trim build, but he wasn’t one of those drop-dead, super-hero, six-pack hotties. He was more Bruce Banner than Thor. Still hot, only on a different scale. Even so, I could sit there all day and listen to him talk. I couldn't say the same about Thor.

"Um, yeah. Fine. Although, I'm getting mine to go. I have a lot on my plate today."

"Me too," he said with a smile.

For a moment, we just sat there, not saying anything.

"So, how is Tripod?" I asked, relieved to have a topic of discussion.

"Tripod?"

"The kitten. The one with only three good legs now thanks to you." He smirked in approval of the name.

"The vet is taking a look at her today. He hopes it's just broken, but he might have to amputate it."

"Poor, Tripod," I said, making a face of my own. "Did you figure out whose cat it was?"

Scott shook his head. "Stan, the vet, thinks it was probably the runt of a litter, based on its size. He said if we hadn't found it, chances were good it would have starved to death."

"Good thing you hit it then."

That garnered another killer grin from him.

My cell buzzed beside me, rattling loudly against my spoon and startling me. Embarrassed, I quickly scooped it off the table to silence it but not before I caught a glimpse of the sender's name on the text.

Hey, sexy. The wife and the kids are going to the movies at 2 today. Stop by so we can—

I didn't finish reading Anthony's invite. Clearly, he didn't know I'd left town yet. He'd figure it out soon enough. Still, my fingers ached to message him a curt reply. Secretly, I wanted him to know I had left. I still wanted him to care.

"Something wrong?" Scott said.

I shoved the phone inside my back pocket.

"Nope. I'm good."

Thankfully, our coffees arrived just then. I took a greedy sip ignoring the foamy burn. Scott grabbed his paper cup and then stood.

"Well, I won't keep you," he said. "Thanks again for your help this morning."

"Sure. Anytime you run over a cat, I'm your girl."

I winced internally at my lame-ass comeback as he waved and walked out of the coffee shop. My eyes followed him as he left. As they did, I also noticed other customers watching me. Not just one or two, but almost every eye was on me. *Right.* Almost forgot about that pesky doppelganger problem.

"Can I get you anything else?" I glanced up, and another waitress was standing beside me, pen in hand. She was young, in her twenties. Perky breasts, straight teeth, short, choppy black hair. I hated her instantly. I wanted my other waitress back.

"Oh, I already ordered," I said, lifting my cup.

"Yeah, Sandy thought you might like something to eat too, but she was too nervous to ask if you had wanted anything else."

"Nervous?" I asked.

"Well, yeah, I mean, it's not every day a movie star walks into our town, let alone our coffee shop."

I closed my eyes.

"I'm not her."

Little Ms. Betty Boop winked at me. "Sure, you're not."

"I'm not. Honest. My name is Julie Green. Jules for short."

She smiled as though in secret understanding. "Right. *Jules*. You're secret is safe with me."

My hand reached up to pinch my brow. “Look, can I just get an everything bagel with cream cheese.”

Her eyes lit up “Oh, sure. It’s on the house.” She beamed.

I started to protest but thought about my limited funds.

“Can you also make it to go,” I clarified. I wasn’t about to stay in this fish bowl any longer than necessary.

“Anything for you Morgan—I mean Jules,” she said, winking at me.

I left a few minutes later with my bagel and coffee, wondering just how I was going to start my life over when the entire town already thought they knew who I was?

Chapter 5

With my head down low to avert the onlookers that keep cropping up as I walked farther into town, I took the last bites of my bagel and tried, discreetly, to fish out the poppy seeds from between my teeth. Those pesky things were delicious but also a pain in the ass to unlodge.

I tossed my bag in the trash can which looked as though it had been freshly painted as there wasn't a speck of dirt on it. *Christ, even the garbage around here is clean.*

After walking up and down the streets a few times, it became apparent that because it was Sunday, many of the businesses were closed. A rarity in Los Angeles. The city closed for no one, but here it seemed to be the norm. It made my whole intention job searching a bit of a moot point.

I took out my cell as I walked and stared at the text from Anthony.

Don't answer him. Don't answer him.

Well, maybe just a quick reply.

I'm not coming over. Ever again. I'm done. Goodbye.

With a quick breath, I turned the phone off. I knew he would reply when he saw the message, and I wasn't feeling quite strong enough to deal with that at the moment.

Seeing as there was no point in hanging around town, I opted to go home and bury myself in the covers for the day and start over tomorrow.

While crossing the street, I tried to convince myself I was grumpy because I'd bothered to put pants on and venture out into the real world today, but I knew it was the text message that was weighing heavy on my mind.

I was thinking of all the things I'd been building my courage to say to Anthony when he found out what I had done. I had an epic speech all planned out. I was busy practicing the lines in my head when I saw the lady from the supermarket up ahead on the sidewalk. The Sticky Kid lady. Her child was booger-free at the moment but appeared extremely unhappy in his fancy clothes. Stray blonde wisps danced around his face as he held the hand of a man I presumed was his father.

"Oh, my goodness, Hank. There she is. That's Morgan Malone! I told you I saw her." The man glanced up at me, bored at first, but then his expression changed to interest. They started to walk toward me.

Shit.

I didn't want to talk to either of them or try to explain yet again, that I wasn't Morgan Malone. I had a feeling they wouldn't believe me no matter what I said. I don't handle confrontation well, so I darted up the stairs leading into a building to my left before they could reach me. A few other people were entering the building, so I tried to hide myself behind the mini crowd. Ducking my head low, I climbed the steps, eager to get inside.

Glancing over my shoulder, I saw that the woman had paused, looked my direction, but then stalked off with the rest of her family and out of my line of sight. I let out a small sigh of relief.

"Well, good morning, Julie."

I looked up and hated the twitch my stomach made when I noticed the silver-eyed fox himself, Scott. He was standing at the door, beaming down at me.

"Um. Hi," I said, hating the butterflies that began to flutter as I stood there. I rubbed at my arms to play down the awkwardness I felt.

"I know, it's a brisk morning, isn't it? The heat's on inside. Go get yourself warm," he said, gesturing inside.

"Inside?" I glanced into the darkened room wishing I'd paid more attention to the building I'd approached.

"I'm glad you could come. Surprised, but glad." His smile grew wider.

"Yeah, me too," I said. Not sure of what else I was supposed to say, I continued walking inside, squinting in the shadows, praying I wasn't walking into some AA meeting or cult worship.

Remembering Scott was still there, I opened my eyes back up to see what he was holding. He smiled and handed me a folded sheet of paper as he led me inside.

I glanced down at the flyer. CPR and You. Learn the basics: Save a Life. *Oh, hell, no. I had wandered into a first aid class?* I peered inside and saw on a table, a fake body and a few random chairs scattered around with about five other people.

"Have a seat up front. Those chairs have cushions on them," He patted the back of a plain, folding metal chair beside me. "Trust me, this guy is hard."

My eyes widened at the unintended innuendo, enjoying the color of red creeping up his neck.

"What I meant was—" he began to blunder.

I smirked but saved him from himself. "I knew what you meant. Still funny."

His cheeks burned scarlet as he squirmed. "I'm just gonna go welcome some more people now," he mumbled while walking back where he'd been standing, greeting people as they came in.

I decided to slink into one of the hard chairs in the back. There was no way I was going to sit at the front of the room, comfy cushions or not. In fact, I was going to sneak out the first chance I got. Sitting in the back was the least conspicuous way to do that.

Promptly at ten, the doors closed out the morning sun, and other stragglers took their seats. I eyed the empty chair next to me, secretly hoping Scott might sit there, but he didn't. Instead, he walked down the aisle toward the front. He was going for the soft seats. I frowned feeling slightly rejected. But he didn't sit there either. He kept walking.

Around the table and behind the dummy. Well, shit. He was the teacher. *Of course.*

"Welcome to CPR training. I'm your instructor, Scott Jacobs. This course is free and is being provided through a grant from the Earl Mathews Foundation. I will be teaching CPR here during the next four weeks, and each class builds on the next, so I highly encourage you to come to each session. You can't get the certification without attending them all and scoring high enough on the final exam." I saw his eyes scan the small group, smiling only when his eyes found mine. My idiotic heart leapt.

Maybe I'd stick around for a few minutes. I could give a rat's ass about learning CPR, but there wasn't anything wrong with admiring the view.

Chapter 6

I sat through the lecture, watching his lips move, but not actually hearing a damn thing he said. Instead, I just watched, ever intent, as he bent over the dummy and pressed his lips to the plastic ones. I'd never wanted to be a hunk of rubber in all my life.

Naturally, the dummy was a dude. His little half-body cut off just before the good bits that would have likely been aroused by the way Scott's hands worked over the fake chest. *Sigh.* It wasn't fair. Why were all men I found attractive unavailable? They were always either uninterested, married, or gay. The married thing apparently did little to deter me, I'm ashamed to admit, but the gay thing I could do something about… like leave.

I stood at the exact moment the class seemed to be dismissed and took that as a sign I had been right to go.

Before I could escape, Scott approached me.

"You stayed." He smiled. "I figured you'd have snuck out by now."

I grimaced, annoyed he'd pegged my intentions to bail correctly.

"What can I say? You give good instructions." I shrugged.

That earned me a smile. "Here, let me walk you out," he said, extending his hand toward the door.

I tried not to absorb the feel of his hand on my lower back as he walked with me to the exit. I tried. Really hard. I failed.

"Will you come again next week?" he asked.

I made a face. "Actually, I'm not very coordinated and would probably just end up causing more damage to anyone I tried to rescue, but I learned a lot. Thanks." I couldn't tell him I only entered his class to escape an annoying woman and not because of my keen interest in saving lives.

Coming from the sidewalk below, I heard a rush of buzzed voices as soon as we stepped outside. A group of people had gathered. They were all surrounding a big black stretch limo.

"Your ride?" I joked.

He let out a slow laugh. "Not on my salary. I wonder if it's for a wedding? There's a church not far from here. Maybe they're lost?"

Scott walked down the stairs, and I followed him, not to go with him but to get my ass home. I was ready to take off these stupid shoes.

Before I could get onto the sidewalk, however, the front door of the limo opened up, and a chauffeur stepped out. A massive black man, decked on in a black suit, and sunglasses. Very *Men in Black* looking. He opened the back door, waiting for someone to get in or out.

The crowd watched for the mysterious guest to appear, but when no one got out, a few people glanced at me.

"It's not mine," I said, trying to rush past. The chauffeur moved his body to step in front and stopped me with his intimidating presence.

"Ms. Malone, please get into the car," the man said. Standing next to me, I noticed he was twice my size. This guy could pass for a bouncer in any bar in the city.

"Oh, I'm not her. Nice car, though."

I tried to leave again, but his wrist wrapped around mine.

"I've been instructed to use force, if necessary," he whispered. "Please, just get into the limo."

The hushed voices around me grew louder as I saw Scott gawk up at me, clearly confused.

"But I'm not—"

The man glared as though challenging me. I had the sneaking feeling I'd already lost whatever fight I would have gotten into with him.

"Fine. I'll take the lift, but you are making a huge mistake." I started laughing. This was insanity, but I wasn't going to win an argument with this giant so might as well enjoy the ride while it lasted.

I climbed into the car and slid easily onto the massive leather seats. My body sunk into the cushion, absorbing its luxurious softness with delight. After an hour on the folding chair, this was heaven on my ass. My hands brushed against the soft material, checking around at the opulent display of wealth. The limo my friends and I had hired on prom night a gazillion years ago had nothing on this thing.

The door closed, and the world outside was shut out. Through the windows, I found Scott standing among the rest of the onlookers. He wore an expression of utter confusion.

"This ought to be fun to explain." I giggled, enjoying the moment the confusion brought. I'd let Scott know the truth soon enough, but for now, I was grateful for the mix-up. So were the blisters on my pinky toes.

I laid my head against the seatback and sighed.

"You know I'm not really her, right?" I said to the driver as he got in and turned the key.

He didn't answer and started driving.

"I live at the top of that hill there," I said, pointing as though telling a cabbie. "A small yellow cape. Big black SUV in the drive. Cat blood on the road in front of it." I smirked. "Can't miss it." I closed my eyes, still enjoying the feel of the leather. *I could get used to this.*

When I realized the car had turned left instead of staying straight, I opened one eye. "Um, this is not the way. I'm up the hill," I said, sitting up.

"I have my instructions," was his only reply.

I slid across the seat to get closer to the open window that separated us.

"Look, buddy, you need to stop this car now. This is kidnapping. I'm not Morgan Malone." I dug inside my purse to pull out my driver's license, but I couldn't find it. "Dammit. Okay, so I can't prove it at the moment, but my name is Julie Green. I'm from LA, and I live in a house just up the road. Please, this is a big misunderstanding. I am not famous."

"That is none of my concern, Ms. Green. I'm just doing my job."

I scoffed. "Your job? To pick up some random stranger and abduct them?"

"The car phone is about to ring," he said, with no trace of emotion on his face. "I would suggest you answer it."

"The car pho—" No sooner had I begun the sentence than a phone, that wasn't mine, rang.

I glanced at the driver who pushed a button and the privacy window closed. Seeing no other way to get any answers, I picked up the cell from the seat beside me.

"Hello?"

"Is this Julie? Julie…shit, what was her last name?" I heard papers shuffling around, "Green. Julie Green?"

"Um, yes. Who is this?" I asked, trying to place where I'd heard the voice before.

"Well, this is Morgan Malone, of course."

Chapter 7

The limo continued to move as my eyes stared blankly out the back window. I was talking to a movie star. I was in her car. Morgan Malone knew who I was. This wasn't real. This sort of thing didn't happen in the real world.

"So, listen, Julie," she began.

"Jules. Call me Jules."

There was a pause and then, "Okay, fine, Jules. Here's the thing. I had Bernard track you down. It was actually really easy to find you once you got into Bucksville because all it takes is one post on social media saying I was there, when I'm not, to nail your location. Bernard asked a few people and found you." My head tried to keep up with her logic as she rambled on. "It's actually, like fate, or something that you ended up in the town where one of my summer houses is located. Like, kismet, ya know?"

"Um, sure," I said, still very star-struck.

"Look, I'll level with you. Something's come up, and I find that I am currently…unavailable for public consumption."

I shifted in my seat. "Sorry to hear that." *What the hell was Morgan Malone doing on the phone with me?*

"Trust me, this was soooo not planned. Anywho, my idea had originally been to just disappear until this *issue* blew over, but then I caught wind that people were starting to mistake you for me. At first, I was annoyed. The last thing I needed was to be compared to some random loser—"

Nice. Even to Rich and the Famous, I was a loser.

"But then I thought, 'Hey, this could work out great.'"

"What could work out? Will someone please tell me what's going on?" I was getting pretty annoyed at this point.

The limo slowed and pulled up a long winding driveway. A massive compound of a house came into view.

"Whoa, where are we?" I asked more to myself than to anyone.

Morgan laughed. "That would be my getaway house. It's yours for the next three months if you want it, along with a spending allowance and ten thousand dollars when the job is done."

"Wait. What?" The limo door opened, and Bernard was there, waiting for me to get out.

"Fine. Twenty-five thousand," Morgan huffed. "Go on, take a look around. Tell me the place isn't for you, and I'll withdraw my offer."

Bernard opened the door for me. I got out of the car, utterly confused, and walked up the intricately placed stone steps. The entire building appeared like something out of a magazine with its trimmed hedges, floor-to-ceiling windows, and a sprawling building footprint.

I stopped walking. "No. I'm not going in there. I need you to tell me what's going on. This is insanity."

"Fine. But I need you to sign a nondisclosure form first. Bernard should have one for you."

"A nondis—what?"

At that, Bernard was by my side with a very legal looking paper and a pen.

"It means you won't go blabbing your mouth about what I'm going to tell you," Morgan sighed, clearly annoyed at me.

I looked at the form, and then back at an unsmiling and very serious looking Bernard, and quickly signed it.

"It's signed, Ms. Malone," Bernard said into the phone, snatching the form away and striding up to the door. He waited there like a butler, holding the door for me to go inside.

Morgan let out a slow breath before she spoke. "I'm sick, Jules. Like really sick. I'm in Mexico at some clinic that is supposed to help." She sounded unconvinced. "This place is my last ditch effort to get better. The treatment takes about three months, but if I disappear for that long with a release about to come out, I might not have a life to go back to. The movie world is fickle as a teenager's crush. If I step out of the spotlight, for even a second, I'll get placed on the back burner on people's minds. By that time, directors and screenwriters will have forgotten to think about me, too. I don't want to be forgotten just because this damn skin cancer has decided to try and kill me."

"Skin cancer?" I whispered. Bernard stared at me, but he didn't seem shocked. He must have already known.

Morgan laughed a deep, sarcastic sort of laugh. "I guess fifteen years on a tanning bed wasn't so smart."

"Oh." I plopped to sit on the steps. Why was she telling me all of this? What possible role could I play?

"The cosmetic surgery I had wasn't because I was unhappy with my face. I loved my face. It was done to cover the parts of my face they cut off to remove the cancer."

"Oh, my God." I gasped.

"Yeah. Not fun. Believe me, I had no intentions of trying to turn myself into…well, you."

I frowned and glanced down at the phone for a second. "Gee, thanks."

"Oh, please, don't be so sensitive," Morgan said. I could practically hear her eyes rolling in her head. "The short version is that what they cut off my face was supposed to be the end of it, but it seems that the cancer is now in other places they can't just cut out, so I'm trying some experimental stuff instead."

I sat in shocked silence as I listened to her talk.

"The good news is that my doctors tell me if this treatment works, I should be good as new in a few months, which is great, but until then, I don't want to lose my spot in the limelight. Understood?"

"Um. No. Not at all understood. What are you trying to say?"

Morgan made a disgruntled noise. I envisioned her pinching her brows together with her fingers. It's what I would do.

"I want you to pretend to be me. For three months or so. You can live in my house and spend my money. You don't have to do anything except maybe sign a few autographs and look damn good every time you go out in public, and go wherever my agent says you need to go. She has the schedule. Just show up, smile. It will be easy. Bernard will help you. Just live your life, and make sure people see me, well you. They need to know I haven't fallen off the face of the earth." The sound of the phone shuffled as she talked. "It's easy money. Tell Bernard to give you the contract. Look it over. He can call me with your answer.

I blinked several times, completely dumbfounded by her request. "Wait…you want *me* to pretend to be *you*?"

"Isn't that what I just said?" Morgan sounded annoyed. "Look, I have to go into the treatment room now. Can you just read over the contract? Bernard knows how to reach me." And with that, she hung up.

I stared at the phone for a long time until the limo driver approached and took the cell from me and slid it into the inside pocket of his jacket. He gestured to the door.

"She's insane. She is out of her mind. Did you know about this?" I asked, looking up at the beast of a man.

"Yes, ma'am. I told you I had my instructions."

I shook my head at him. "Well, I'm not doing it. She can kiss my ass. I don't want to be famous, not even pretend-famous. I just want to go home, crawl back into bed and forget this day even happened."

"I'm instructed to show you the house, Ms. Malone."

"Ugh! Don't call me that! You know I'm not her." I said, honestly not wanting anything to do with this.

He didn't skip a beat while opening the door wider. Seeing as how he was my ride home, and I had no idea where I was to try and get there on my own, I saw little choice in the matter. I could walk through her house if that was what it took, but after that, I was going back to mine.

"Fine. Show me the stupid house. After that, you are driving me to my real house."

"Right this way," he said, opening the door wider.

To say that the inside was more stunning than the outside was the understatement of the millennia. Polished hardwood floors shined against the afternoon sun. Crisp white walls with art even I recognized hung in delicate frames so lush looking that they were likely worth more than everything I owned just by themselves. A large sprawling seating area filled with leather sofas and elegant, dainty-looking chairs filled the living area that seemed to go on for days. But it was the trees, *real live trees*, that stretched from the corners of the house and snaked their way upward that stunned me. Their branches reached up to the sky, poking out through holes made in the walls and beyond to some unknown structure that allowed their leaves to thrive. This was the very definition of rich. And I hated that I found myself wondering how living in this home might feel.

"You're to read this before I can drive you back," Bernard said, holding out a thick manila envelope for me.

"I'm not doing it," I said, snatching the papers from him. I plunked down on a cream-colored armchair that was just as comfortable as it looked.

"I'll be by the car when you're ready, ma'am," he said, tipping his shiny black chauffeur's hat and leaving me in the serenity of Morgan Malone's house. My house, if I so desired.

Taking a breath, I opened the small metal clasp on the envelope and began to read the terms of what it would actually mean to play Morgan Malone's doppelganger.

Chapter 8

I heard Bernard enter the house, but I didn't look up from the contract.

"The maids will be arriving within the hour to tend to the house, and your agent will be here later as well," Bernard said, walking into the room where I had been reading the stack of paperwork for the last several minutes. He stood there, hovering before he cleared his throat. "Well?"

"Well, what?" I said, glancing up from the paper I was reading.

"Have you come to a decision as to whether or not you shall assume Ms. Malone's identity?" He said it with such normalcy that it was almost impossible to hear the idiotic nature of his statement.

"I—I can't. There is just no way. I mean, first off, no one would believe it," I said, as though that settled the matter.

Bernard eyed me as he pulled out his cell, swiped the screen a few times and then held it out to me. "They already have."

Confused, I stared at the phone. On it was a picture of me…talking on the phone with Morgan, just outside this house, not thirty minutes ago. The caption under the photo read: Morgan Malone spotted taking refuge in her New Hampshire mansion.

"How the hell? Who took this picture?"

Bernard reached for his phone and tucked it into the breast of his suit jacket.

"I did. As were my orders. Ms. Malone needed to be found someplace other than where she *really* was."

I stood up, feeling ridiculously betrayed. "What? You took a photo of me, sent it to the media, and told them I was her?"

"Yes." He locked his hands firmly in front of himself, immovable in his emotion.

"But what if I said no?" I shrieked.

"Have you?" he asked.

"I'll mess it up…" I said in my softest voice. I couldn't even believe I had been considering it. It was ridiculous, preposterous, and yet…all that money, for just living in this house and pretending awhile. That much cash would afford me the sort of do-over I needed to help me forget all about Anth—what's his name.

"I'll make sure you don't mess anything up." He took a step closer to me. "One thing we need to be clear on, though. The three of us are the only people who know about this arrangement, and that's how it needs to stay. You can't breathe a word of this, to anyone, or it breaches the contract. Trust me, you don't want Morgan's legal team riding your ass. She can afford the best."

"But people already know who I am. People who know I moved here…" I protested.

"Who specifically?" He got out a pad of paper and pushed out a small pencil that lived inside the wire binding.

"Well, just my best friend, Macy, actually. She doesn't know what town I'm in, but she knows I came to the east coast." I bit my lip. "But Macy noticed how much Morgan looked like me, so my cover is already blown."

"And where does this Macy live?" he said without skipping a beat.

"LA."

He jotted it down. "And her last name?"

"Watts. Why?" I asked while walking over to him.

"Who else knows you're here?"

I crossed my arms. "Um, the locals."

"You mean the ones who already think you're Morgan Malone?"

I shook my head, "Yeah, but I've told a lot of them that I'm not her."

"And they believed you?" he countered.

I paused. "Oh, well, not really. Not yet."

He closed his pad. "Good. Easy enough to explain that away. You were trying to have some peace and quiet. Didn't want people to make a fuss."

He jotted down a few more notes.

"Anyone else? Siblings? Parents?"

"I'm an only child. My dad moved away when I was young, and we haven't heard from him since. I told my mother I was on a temp job where there wasn't great cell service, which she probably won't buy, but it might give us some time to come up with a better story."

"How about boyfriends?"

I shook my head. "I don't have a boyfriend."

"Any ex's know you're here."

My mind flashed to Anthony without meaning to. I hated myself for wondering if he'd read my text yet, if he had replied or not. *Would he be angry? Would he try to find me? Or just forget all about me?*

"Well?" he asked, showing impatience.

"No. No one knows I'm here except Macy."

"No one else? You're sure?"

I shook my head. I don't know why I didn't mention Scott. He was the only one here who knew my real identity, and yet, I didn't want to sick Bernard on him. I was never gonna see him again anyway, so it really didn't matter.

Bernard closed his pad and tucked it into his breast pocket. "Don't tell anyone else you're here. Understood? I'll deal with Macy."

I scoffed. "And just how do you plan to do that?" My eyes widened suddenly. "You're not going to kill her are you?"

Bernard glared at me. "No."

"Well, then how? Macy is pretty stubborn when she wants to be. She doesn't like to be told what to do by anyone."

"If you're doing this, you need to go and get changed," he said, ignoring my question "Your room is the last door on the left."

I gaped at him, speechless.

"Pick anything from her closet and burn what you're wearing," he said. "Morgan would never allow her help to see her like…" he gestured at me. "Well…you."

I frowned at Bernard as he handed me a pen to sign the contract. I hadn't really read all of it, but what harm could I do living in this cushy house for a few months while I pampered myself? It would mean I could put off my job hunt for at least a while until my head was firmly screwed on. It almost seemed as though this opportunity was being handed to me from the universe. Throwing caution to the wind, I signed on the dotted line and hoped for the best.

After kicking off my painful sandals, I made my way toward my new room, marveling at how warm the smooth wood floors were on bare feet. I bet Morgan had heated floors throughout this entire place. Closing my eyes, I smiled at how good it felt on my toes. Oh, I could get used to this.

I really wanted to just plunk down on a bed and go back to sleep after the morning I'd had, but I had been assigned another job. For now, my task was to change clothes. I paused for a moment, realizing the request to change went beyond the clothes. My job was to slip on more than her clothes; I needed to wear her entire life for a while. I had reached a new level of insane.

"What am I doing?" I asked my feet as they turned into Morgan's bedroom. Any thoughts about whether I would go through with this ruse or not changed when I saw her room.

Cream colored everything greeted me, along with the largest bed I had ever seen. It was literally as if someone had put two king mattresses together. The furniture was massive, and yet, the room still had ample space inside. Why would one person need that much tossing and turning space?

I tiptoed into the room, feeling as if I was invading an off-limits area. Going into someone's bedroom was a very intimate thing. I always thought that a bedroom spoke the most truth about who you were, which was probably why I never allowed anyone in mine. Not even Anthony. If we had sex, it was on the couch or the floor, or a hotel room, but never on my bed. I knew the idea was all very *Pretty Woman* of me with the no kissing on the mouth thing, but it was my rule. I told boyfriends it was because having sex in my bedroom was too *vanilla*, but really, I just didn't want any of them stepping into my universe. I had to protect my heart, especially with Anthony. At least, until he left his wife, which I know now was just the line he fed me to keep me caged. *God, how pathetic had I been?*

Not anymore. Now I get to step completely out of that life and begin again with a brand new and exciting one including servants and meals not from a take-out menu, not to mention a bed the size of the Titanic. Yeah, I could do that for a few months. And afterward, I could reinvent myself. Move to London, Italy, wherever. The only part that mattered was this temp gig actually offered me options.

If I had said no, all that would have been waiting for me was the rental I couldn't afford and a life with no future. The Morgan option was a financially sound decision. My mom would be proud…even if I couldn't tell her.

That got me to thinking I should probably text her again now that this gig was going to be a few months long. Maybe while I was texting, I could sneak a peek to see if Anthony had replied as well.

I reached into my back pocket to grab the cell, except it wasn't there. I frowned and spun around as though thinking it must have miraculously slid out of my pocket without me feeling it. Then, panic hit. Had I lost it in town? If anyone found it, they'd realize I wasn't really Morgan Malone. They'd see my photos in LA; they'd see my social media pages; they'd see…oh, God. *The video I made for Anthony one stupidly drunk night.* I turned green.

"Bernard!" I shrieked running out of the bedroom. "We need to go back into town, now!"

I found him standing in the doorway, his hands clasped in front of him, a dark and immovable force. His eyes flicked calmly to me, unfazed by my frantic running.

"My cell phone!" I panted. "I think I lost my cell phone in town, and we have to go back. We have to get it. There's proof on there about who I really am and—"

Bernard casually dug into his jacket and pulled out my phone.

"Hey, that's mine," I said, staring blankly at him. "How did you get it?"

"You left it in the limo," he said before he returned it to his pocket.

"Well, give it back."

"No. No calls from your cell during your time here. It was part of the contract. No connection with the outside world."

"But, my mom and Macy. They'll worry about me if I don't message them," I said, which was actually quite sad that they would be the only two people who would care if I vanished for a few months or not.

"You'd be surprised what a few sunny beach Wish You Were Here postcards will do. It establishes that you are well and out of touch, which is just what we want."

I cocked my head considering the simple beauty of the idea. Still, it didn't help my current predicament. "Look, I need to delete something on there…something private."

He hesitated for a moment.

"Fine, but do it here in front of me. I can't risk you jeopardizing our arrangement."

I nodded in agreement as he tentatively handed me the phone. It only took a few swipes to delete the video. I was about to return it, but I just had to check the text messages.

"Almost done," I said.

Bernard's eye's narrowed as I switched to my text messages. Anthony had replied.

Don't do this, baby. You know I love you. This pregnancy just complicates things, but I will leave her. You know I will. I just…just need some time to break the news to her. Let me make this up to you. Please, baby. She'll be at a school field trip. We can have the day…

I could actually feel myself wanting to believe the lies. It would be so easy to go back. But I knew nothing would change if I did. Not really. I closed my eyes and deleted the text.

"All done," I whispered.

Bernard snatched the phone.

"Now, please. Go change. We have much to discuss before your staff arrives."

He pointed down the hall, and like an obedient dog, I went back to the bedroom.

Chapter 9

Living in LA for as long as I had, there was no way to avoid knowing a thing or two about fashion. The place was a melting pot of those who didn't care, those with poor taste, those whose styles were clearly meant to impress someone but fell flat, and then there were the truly opulent when it came to style. I fell somewhere between the poor taste and trying to impress. Part of me hated that I'd tried to be trendy like all my friends, and the other part despised the fact that my clothes never seemed to look right on me. There was always a roll that shouldn't be there or a button that was pulled too tightly against its seams.

If I had my way, I would live in a T-shirt and sweatpants, but my job as a temp required me to dress up. So, I put on the heels and the lipstick, just so I could get the paycheck at the end of the week, but it never really *felt* like me. I was never comfortable in my skin. The fact that I could wear jeans and a sweatshirt nonstop if I wanted to had actually been a huge reason for moving here. I was going to be able to live the simple life that I'd seen in the magazines and online. Flannels, jeans, and boots were hip here. I could get down with that.

When I opened Morgan's closet, I shouldn't have been surprised to see the sheer volume and wealth laid out in color-coded patterns before me, but I was. Not one of them looked like it held a sweatshirt.

The sheer size of the closet had my mouth hanging open in shock. It's one thing to see a famous person's huge closet on TV, but it is quite another to be standing in the middle of it, knowing you have to try and cram your fat ass into them.

I stood there, frozen, for several moments, mouth agape turning in small circles staring at the volume of shoes, hats, dresses, and bags. Two large dressers on either end of the closet held even more stuff. What else could Morgan possibly have in there?

"Do you need some assistance?" I heard Bernard's deep voice say behind me. I jumped and turned to look at him, a hand clasped over my heart.

"God, don't do that!" I shrieked.

Bernard blinked at me slowly.

"Morgan doesn't shriek. Morgan is very calm when she's at this house. It's her downtime house, a place where she can be more herself. That said, the first few days, the staff knows she will be *off*. It takes Morgan a few days get out of her LA bitchy rich mode and back into the body she was born to so we can work your transition in that way. However, we do need you to start behaving as much like her as humanly possible. The clothes are only the beginning. Put something on so we can move on to the next item," he directed.

"But, I have no idea what to pick. There are way too many options! I don't know even if any of this will fit! I mean, we may have the same face but our bodies—"

"Are quite similar," Bernard finished, brushing past me to open the dresser I hadn't dared open. Inside were neatly folded sweaters. Naturally. He pulled out a thin black one, draped it over his arm, and spun around and picked out a white button-down shirt with tiny gold zigzagging lines. He scooted farther into the massive closet to pull off the skinniest pair of dark blue jeans I'd ever seen and added it to his pile.

Walking over to the shoes, he paused for a moment and settled on a pair of tan colored mega heels before coming back to stand in front of me.

"You'll wear this. Undergarments are in the other dresser. Spanx will be your best friend for the next three months." He smiled then nodded in the direction of my head. "Wear your hair up in a high bun. No jewelry. This is a typical relaxation outfit for Morgan.

I glanced down at the heels. "Morgan relaxes in heels?"

Bernard seemed completely exasperated by me. "When you spend your entire life in heels, it affects your arches. Wearing anything else once your feet are trained to wear them actually hurts, so yes, heels are more comfortable to Morgan than your…" he said, glancing down at my own shoes still in my hand, "sandals."

"Hey, these are comfy," I lied, wondering if the blister on my pinky toe was showing.

"Well, they wouldn't be for Morgan. Get changed. Meet me in the screening room when you're finished." Without another glance, he walked past me.

"Um, where's that?"

Bernard stopped but didn't turn around. The tension in his shoulders gave away the apprehension he was feeling about making this plan successful.

"Go right and up the stairs. Look for the blue leather sofas."

I snickered. "*Blue* leather couches?"

He turned around to look at me. "Naturally. It's Morgan's—your favorite color."

"Ah."

And with that, the big man left me holding the clothes.

Thirty minutes later, I had managed to wiggle my girdled butt into the jeans that had a weird-ass slit in the front part of each leg. At first, I thought they were torn, but when I noticed the meticulous stitching, I knew I was just getting lesson one in highbrow fashion. An ugly one.

In her bathroom, Morgan had a gold-tinted vanity set up with makeup and lotions. I sat in the blue chair and looked at myself in the mirror. I wasn't normally a makeup kind of girl, though I did know how to apply it. Anthony liked the look on me, so I had taught myself to please him. I growled. *Stop thinking about him.*

As I used her brush to fix my hair, I noticed she had several pictures of herself scattered around the vanity. Red carpet sort of shots, and the type of vain pictures you'd expect a celebrity to have of themselves, but there was one, sort of hidden behind a large bottle of hair product, that caught my eye. I pulled out the frame and saw Morgan in an outfit similar to the one I was now wearing…hair up in the bun…Bernard at her side, smiling together sitting on the couch in the living room. I'd never seen Bernard smile. Or, for that matter, Morgan, come to think of it. In all the pictures I'd seen of her in the press, she hadn't shown a smile. Her on-camera expression was always a very somber Posh Spice sort. Pouty lips, serious eyes. But here, in this picture with Bernard, a large black man who nearly dwarfed her, she seemed…happy. Relaxed. They both did.

A light bulb went off in my head. Bernard was more than just a driver to Morgan. He liked her. That would explain why he was so intent on making this plan work.

I replaced the photo, feeling as though I had trespassed on a memory I wasn't meant to see.

Dutifully, I pulled my hair up in the desired bun before I began the painstakingly long task of putting on makeup to have it appear as though I was wearing none. A light layer of lip gloss finished the desired effect, which meant I had stalled long enough. I had to put on those heels now. I was no stranger to heels, though the ones I wore for work were a few inches shorter. This stiletto thing was for the birds.

I crammed my sore pinkies into the shoe and stood up straight, waiting for the pain to take over, but it didn't. They actually didn't feel that bad, almost…comfortable. "For five hundred dollars, I suppose they should be comfortable," I muttered as I left the bedroom and made my way up to find Bernard.

The blue leather couches greeted me in the dim glow of a TV screen that was turned on. Bernard was there, fiddling with the controls when I walked in.

"Does this look okay?" I asked, afraid I wasn't going to pass for Morgan even a little bit.

He looked up from the remotes and stared, mouth slightly open for a moment before he composed himself. His quick smirk was enough to confirm two things: One, I passed for Morgan. Two, Bernard had a thing for her. What I didn't know for sure was if the feelings went both ways.

"Pull the collar out of the sweater, and frown a bit more, and you'll pass for her for sure," he said.

I did as instructed as he handed me the remotes.

"You need to watch these tapes. They're of Morgan at events. Observe how she gestures, walks, talks, anything you can."

I glanced down at the couch and back at Bernard.

"You seem to be going out of your way for Morgan," I said casually. "I thought drivers just drove the stars' cars."

Bernard frowned. "I'm not Morgan's driver."

"Oh?" I asked sheepishly.

"I'm her bodyguard."

It was my turn to frown. "Oh. Right." Not exactly the answer I was expecting, but I supposed it made sense. At least it accounted for his sheer size and his general lack of smiling and interest in all things Morgan. Then again, there was that picture…

As much as I would have rather dug deeper into Bernard's backstory, there was another one I needed to learn: Morgan's, and I needed to do it fast. I shoved my curiosity aside for the moment and hunkered down to learn about my new life as Bernard went downstairs to prepare for the cleaning crew's impending arrival.

Chapter 10

I sat with eyes glued to the screen and tried to replicate Morgan's expressions. It actually wasn't too hard since the pouty lip was all she ever seemed to wear. It was a simple matter of remembering to keep my bottom lip pushed out more than I normally did…basically looking bored. Bored and pouty. I could do that for three months if it meant free room and board at this joint. Not to mention the payout.

I closed my eyes and leaned back against the softness of the couch. Morgan had good taste. So far, everything I had sat on here felt divine compared to the lumpy couch at home. *Home.*

Shit. My stuff. My lease. My rental. I had to get those squared away if I was going to stay here.

I pushed off the couch and went down the stairs, almost falling ass over tea kettle in the shoes. I stopped dead when I reached the landing. Bernard was there, talking to a crew of five people.

Bernard met my gaze for half a second, but it was enough to let me know he was annoyed I had come downstairs. Clearly, I had messed up on my first attempt at being Morgan.

The housekeeping staff, who either didn't seem to notice my arrival on the stairs like a drunk rhino, or were trained well enough to ignore my presence, stayed focused on Bernard who was giving them instructions.

"Your orders are as normal for vacation stay protocols. Ms. Malone needs this place to be her sanctuary. She requires quiet and to be left undisturbed. Is that understood?"

Uniform bobbing of hair-netted heads nodded in unison. The group broke apart and divided without communication. None of them so much as looked up at me when they went to their assigned rooms. Not even the maid who passed me on the way up the stairs with her bucket of cleaning supplies acknowledged my existence. She merely hugged the banister opposite me as close as she could, as though afraid to touch me.

After the staff had scattered, I cleared my throat.

"Bernard, bring the car around," I said as casually, as I could, knowing one of them may overhear this conversation.

He focused on me, one eyebrow raised, but nodded and left to get the car. I grinned at my newfound power.

Once I slid into the car, thankful for the dark tint, I suddenly felt very exposed outside of the house now that the world knew I was staying there. I had read about how sneaky the paparazzi were, and I didn't want to be caught picking out a wedgie or something equally as embarrassing.

As soon as the car door shut, Bernard lowered the window between us.

"Mind telling me what's going on?" he asked.

"I have loose ends to tie up. I have to call my landlord, return the rental—"

He sighed. "I'm going to take care of that for you. I told you this already. I have a list of calls to make today. Now can we go back inside?"

"Oh, um, well." I felt a little foolish making him come out to the car just to go back inside again. "Can I at least go back to the house and get some of my things?"

"Tell me what you require. I'll arrange for it to be brought here," he said, shifting to stare at me in the rearview mirror.

"I don't know what I *require,"* I said, annoyed. "Just drive me there, please. Let me look around and see what I need. It will take five minutes."

"And what if you are seen?"

I sighed. "Isn't that the point? That people see me here?"

He spun around to look at me through the glass. "In public places, sure, but not at a rental house. Why would Morgan Malone be at a rental house when she has a mansion?"

I blew out a breath. "It's almost nightfall. No one will see me. Come on, you don't intend to keep me locked up in that mansion for three months, do you?" By the set of his eyes, it was clear that was *exactly* what he intended to do.

"Bernard, I'm not going to be held a prisoner in that house. Now, let me get my things," I said firmly.

"Right away, Ms. Malone," he replied. He promptly closed the privacy screen, leaving me alone with my thoughts.

The sun had just started to sink in the sky, its beams bouncing off the trees lining the road. It was absolutely gorgeous. As we drove up and down the winding roads, I marveled at all the beauty here. It was stunning. Peaceful. A far cry from uniform nature of the palm trees and buffed-up beach bodies.

When the limo turned into the driveway, I closed my eyes against the sound of the tires crunching along the white gravel below; it was like a chorus of welcome from the earth itself.

"Make it fast," Bernard said while opening and holding the door for me.

"Right," I said and marched up to the front door.

"Did you bring your keys?" he muttered behind me.

I placed my hand on the door, turned around to face him, and opened it.

His face grew dark. "You didn't lock your house?"

I shrugged. "The landlady hasn't given me the keys yet. She said no one locks their doors here anyway."

Bernard's hand reached instinctively into the back of his pants, and he pulled out a gun.

"Jesus Christ! What the hell are you doing?" I shrieked, sinking back against the house.

"Keep your voice down," he hissed. "Get in the car and lock the door. The glass is bulletproof. Don't unlock the doors until you hear my voice."

"Bernard, no one is in there," I said.

He whipped his head around with a fierce glare.

"Go. Now."

The edge in his voice made me wonder if I *should* worry, so naturally, I did. I ran to the limo, locked the doors as ordered and sat in fear wondering if his bodyguard senses were picking up a *crazed lunatic in my house* sort of vibe.

I watched from my crouched position as Bernard disappeared into the house, preparing myself for the sound of a gunshot or scream something.

That's when there was a knock on the limo window. I screamed and buried my head in my lap. A moment later, I heard Bernard shouting at someone to put his hands up.

"Don't shoot! It's just a kitten," the voice said.

Scott's voice.

Instantly, I flung the door open, saw Scott standing in my driveway, the poor little tiger kitten held up in the air as if she were the unwitting star of *The Lion King*.

"Bernard. Put the gun down. He's a friend," I shouted.

The two men exchanged glances as the bodyguard slowly lowered his gun.

"You know this man?" Bernard said, walking toward me, placing his body between mine and Scott's.

I shoved at Bernard to move, but he was like a rock.

"Ugh, yes, I know him so chillax!"

He grunted down at Scott but eventually took a few steps back.

Scott stood there, the poor kitten still dangling, her tiny cries had me reaching out to cradle her. That's when I noticed her neon pink cast. It covered the length of her entire left leg.

"Awww, you didn't lose your leg?" I said to the cat. "I can't call you Tripod anymore." I rubbed my nose into her soft fur as she nestled against my neck, purring wildly. "Well, maybe I can. You still only have three good legs."

"Sorry, I didn't mean to surprise you," Scott said, keeping a close eye on Bernard. "I just thought you'd want to know that she made it out okay."

I nodded and giggled as the kitten's tongue licked my nose. It was rough and scratchy, yet wonderful all at the same time.

"So this *was* your limo?" Scott asked, his eyebrows raised.

"Oh, right. That," I said, tripping over my words.

"Ms. Malone was just picking up a few of her personal items before heading back to her mansion. She was staying here while it was being fumigated. Now the work is over, she can move back."

I looked at Bernard who had created an impressive cover story for me.

“Miss Malone?” Scott asked. “I thought your last name was Green?”

“Yeah, about that—” My throat tightened. Here it was: time for me to play my part, but looking up into those beautiful silver eyes, I wasn’t convinced I could do it.

Chapter 11

Scott was still standing there, waiting for an explanation—waiting to comprehend why I may have lied to him about who I was. Bernard stepped in and saved the day again, a task I assumed he was well-versed at having to do with Morgan.

"Julie Green is her alias. One of the many she goes by. Being famous has its drawbacks, especially when you are on vacation and trying to relax." Bernard holstered his weapon. "Thanks to the paparazzi discovering she was here, however, she can no longer do that. We need to get you back to the mansion."

I risked a quick glance up at Scott who seemed perplexed.

"Wait, you're famous?"

"This is Morgan Malone," Bernard said in such a way as to try and deliberately insult Scott's intelligence.

By the expression on his face, though, he still didn't know who that was.

"She's an actress. *I'm* an actress," I added quickly. I didn't dare back to look at Bernard, afraid he'd gut me like a pig right then and there for the slip-up.

"An actress? Like in Hollywood?" Scott said, still confused.

"You don't get out much, do you?" I laughed.

Scott's face reddened. He scratched at the back of his head, clearly embarrassed. "Apparently not."

The kitten began squirming in my arms, clearly done with being held and wanting to get down to play.

"Hey, why don't we go inside and talk, and let Tripod here run around awhile."

Bernard took a step forward, "Ms. Malone, we really don't have time—"

"It's fine, Bernard. You can wait outside for me," I said without looking at him, though feeling his eyes burn into the back of my skull. Scott hovered in the driveway for a minute before he followed.

Closing the door behind me, I put down the frisky kitten, who instantly began sniffing around the piles of boxes and loose items, seemingly trying to decide which ones she could climb with her injured leg. She was so adorable hobbling around the floor, I almost couldn't stand it.

"Wow," Scott said, walking around the small living room. He paused at the laundry bin full of stuff I had yet to unpack. "I guess you had to get out in a hurry."

"Oh, yeah. Well, you don't mess around when it comes to termites," I lied.

"Termites? Really? This far north?"

My eyes widened. "You know, I don't really know what bug it was. I just heard bug and was out of there." That actually sounded believable.

"So, you're a movie star?" Scott asked, still looking around the rental that did not scream rich and famous.

It was time to start coming up with a damn good backstory. I figured I would stay as close to the truth as possible so I might have hopes of remembering it. "Um, yeah. I'm surprised you don't recognize me. Everyone else in this damn town seems to."

"They do?"

I shrugged. "I've been in the tabloids recently… I had a few corrective surgeries." I touched my chin for good measure. "It's caused a bit of an uproar. Have you seriously not seen them? They're everywhere."

"I don't read the tabloids." He appeared apologetic for not being up with the times. I suppose his work schedule didn't allow much leisure time. And what little time he had, he probably spent with Liam.

"Right," I said, trying to clear the mental picture of Scott and Liam together from my mind. "Well, you would have found out eventually." I paced slowly around the room as I tried to come up with my next thoughts, using the couch to hide as much as possible from the lies. "Anyway, the tabloids sort of shredded my new look, and I needed to escape the spotlight for a while."

Scott watched me carefully as I paced behind the couch. "Were you horribly disfigured before the surgery?" he asked, clearly not sure he was saying the right thing.

"No, I thought I was beautiful." It wasn't an untrue statement. Morgan was stunning before, but understanding why she had the plastic surgery in the first place sort of negated my feelings. Of course, I couldn't tell Scott about her cancer. It was in violation of the contract. I had to remember that. I had to be careful.

As though reading my mind, I noticed Bernard from the corner of my eye, watching through the window, monitoring my every move, visually warning me to not screw up.

"So, why have the surgery?" Scott paused and lifted Tripod off a pile of clothes she had climbed up but was now stranded too high and couldn't get down. He nuzzled her head with his nose then placed her gingerly on the ground where she hobbled into the other room.

"Um, well, Hollywood isn't that kind to aging actresses. I was getting a lot of pressure from my agent and the studios to dust away a few of the cobwebs." I could see he was buying it, so I went on. "I didn't know the transition would make me look like a completely different person." I picked up a dresser drawer of clothes and moved it to make room on the couch to sit down. Scott did the same on the other end and sat with me. I rubbed my face a few times. "I'm sort of having a mini breakdown actually trying to come to terms with the person staring back at me in the mirror." Also, not an untrue statement.

"I can't imagine what that must be like, having others dictate how you need to look."

I sighed. "It's the job."

Scott focused on me for several minutes, no doubt probably trying to discover the surgical marks on my face, marks that didn't exist on mine, but were instead on the girl who was currently fighting to save her life. "So what are the tabloids saying about your new look?" Scott asked.

"Mostly, that I look horrible. Although, to be fair, even if it had been a vast improvement, the press would still find a way to spin it in a negative light." I shrugged. I reached down to pick up Tripod who was back playing with a ball of crumpled up newspaper. I gave her a few pats on the head, needing her soft little purr to get me through this epic lie.

"Well, they're wrong."

I watched Scott's reaction as Tripod fumbled her way off the couch with a tiny thud.

"Wrong about what?" I asked.

"You look beautiful." I couldn't stop the blush from filling my face. "I can't say if you were more beautiful before the surgery because I didn't know you then, but I can tell you that your face radiates emotion in a way I wouldn't expect from a plastic surgery patient. Not that I've met many people who have had it done," he was quick to add.

"Well, they have come a long way," I said, having no idea what the hell I was talking about. I couldn't think straight. He said I was beautiful. The rest suddenly didn't matter.

Sure, having a gay man flatter me was pointless in the grand scheme of things, but it was also sort of nice to hear. I actually couldn't remember the last time someone, other than my mother, called me beautiful. Not even Anthony used that word. *Sexy* was his term, never beautiful. Hearing Scott use it made me realize the huge difference between the two.

The knock on the door brought me back to my fake reality. "Miss Malone, we really must be going now," Bernard said from outside.

I groaned. "I'm sorry, I was only supposed to be here to grab a couple of things. Bernard isn't a bad guy. He's just doing his job."

Scott stood up. "Well, I suppose he needs to keep you safe from all of us lunatics."

I didn't want Scott to have to go. It was nice talking with him. Life really wasn't fair.

"Now, if only I could find that kitten," he said, looking around the cluttered house.

I saw her little orange tail disappearing into the darkness of my bedroom and had a wicked thought. "Hey, why don't you let her hang out with me at my place awhile? I could use the company. It gets lonely out there since the servants aren't allowed to talk to me." I frowned, wondering if that, in fact, was the truth or not.

"You want me to give you Tripod?" Scott asked. His left eyebrow raised straight to the heavens. "You, the girl who doesn't like cats? Or was that part of the act too?"

I felt the sting of his playful jab.

"Sorry, that came out wrong," he apologized.

Another knock came at the door. This time Bernard popped his head in. "Miss Malone. I must insist. We have to go. You have an appointment with your agent, and you don't want to keep Cassandra waiting."

I glared at him and shooed him away, understanding he was feeding me a line to get Scott out of my house before any paparazzi discovered him there. That would make for an interesting headline: Morgan Malone spotted hanging out with a gay man today…

Ugh. I didn't want to tangle Scott up into this web. It was bad enough that it had ensnared me. "I don't really hate cats. I guess it's more that I've never actually had a pet." He gave me a look of shock. "It's not something I have the time for, so this would just be for a few days or so. Maybe you could pick her up on Friday?"

I was totally using the kitten as an excuse to see Scott again, but I was hoping he wasn't picking up on it.

The corner of his lip raised into a delicious half-smile.

"I could even have Bernard pick you up in the limo," I said, wagging my eyebrows at him.

"Well, far be it for me to turn down a limo ride and a decent week's sleep. Good luck getting any shut-eye with that fur ball chasing after every dust bunny at night."

I gave him a sly grin. "We have a deal. Tell Bernard where you live and have him pick you up, say Friday at noon?"

"Until Friday," Scott said before heading out.

I closed the door behind Scott and watched him walk away to speak to Bernard who seemed confused as to why Scott was giving him his address.

Oh, Jules, what are you doing? Sighing, I grabbed the closest empty container, tucked the kitten inside and made my way out to officially start my new life.

Chapter 12

"What is that thing doing in my car?" Bernard asked once I shut the door.

"Your car? I thought this was Morgan's car?"

Bernard shifted in his seat and glared back at me. "You are not keeping that kitten. Morgan is not a cat person."

I held up Tripod to my nose, and said in a very cutesy voice, "Well it's a good thing I'm not really Morgan."

Bernard huffed. "You *are* Morgan, at least until she gets better. She can't be seen with a kitten."

I frowned and let her down onto the floor to play. "Calm down, Mister Grumpy Pants. I am only borrowing the kitten until Friday."

Bernard's face shifted into a deeper scowl. "About that. Why did you tell that man I'd take him to the mansion? Are you out of your mind?"

"What's the big deal? He's just going to come by and pick up the kitten. Easy peasy."

He scowled and turned back to the wheel. "I'll bring that *thing* back to him. But he's not coming to the mansion."

"Yes, he is. Nothing in the contract mentioned I couldn't have friends."

He started the engine, but I could see his eyes dart at me through the rearview mirror. "Friends you may have. Lovers, no."

I scoffed. "We're not lovers. He's gay." I sighed before admitting that horrible fact.

"For a gay man, he sure seemed interested in your backside," Bernard quipped.

I rolled my eyes. "He probably just liked the cut of my jeans."

"Or the body inside it."

I raised the privacy screen. Bernard didn't know what he was talking about. He hadn't seen Scott and Liam together. And come on, what male nurses do you know that aren't gay? Hell, just the fact that my lady bits tingled when I was near him was confirmation enough that he was out of my league, and batting for the other team was about as far out of the league as you could get. Scott was gay. Of that, I had no doubt.

After a few minutes of stewing, my stomach grumbled. I lowered the window.

"Hey, can we go to a drive-through or something. I'm starving."

Tripod jumped onto the leather seat beside me. Her tiny little claws made holes on the seat, which I tried to cover with my bag.

"We can't. I wasn't lying back there. Your agent is due to arrive in ten minutes."

"What?" I moved across the seats to be closer to the window separating us. "I'm not ready! She'll know who I am! She'll know I'm not Morgan. I can't meet with her. Call it off!"

Bernard didn't answer me for a moment as he maneuvered the limo around a corner. "Trust me, I tried to tell her you were not feeling well, but Cassandra is very persistent. Don't worry, once she sees you in bed, where we will stage the meeting, she won't stay long. I think she just needs to make sure you haven't fallen off the face of the earth."

"But…"

"It'll be fine. I'll be with you the whole time and will speak for you. After all, laryngitis is a terrible affliction." Bernard grinned at me through the rearview mirror.

I sat back in the chair, pondering. "Laryngitis. That's good."

"I know. Now let's get you in bed before Cassandra shows up."

I nodded. "Great idea."

When we pulled into the drive, I heard Bernard curse.

"What's wrong?"

"You took too much time at the house. She's already here," he huffed.

I looked out the window and spotted a red Mercedes parked in front. I whistled low.

"Man, I pay her well."

"Yes, you do."

Tripod began crying, so I picked her up. "What the hell do we do now?"

"Now, you follow my lead." Bernard got out of the car and opened my door before I had a chance to do it myself. I reached to grab the laundry bin of stuff that held my toiletries and undergarments. As I stepped out of the limo with my basket, he stopped me.

"You can't walk into your house with all of that." He grabbed the basket out of my hands and shoved it back in the car. "You need to start thinking like Morgan." A huge sigh escaped his lips as though exasperated by my lack of forethought. "Walk beside me, and don't say a word."

I nodded even though I was terrified. The kitten squirmed in my arms as I followed Bernard into the house.

"And for God's sake, put that *thing* down the moment you get inside," Bernard whispered as he opened the door.

The way Tripod was squirming, I wasn't about to argue. Kittens have surprisingly sharp claws.

At the sound of our arrival, a woman with the shiniest black heels I've ever seen was standing by the couch, one hip perched gently on the edge of it. Cassandra's arms were folded across her chest, obscuring a billowy silk shirt which was tucked neatly into a matching white pencil-cut skirt. Smooth black hair was styled into a severe bob which gave her a look of someone not to be trifled with.

"She lives," Cassandra said, pushing off the couch, her heels clicking across the floor toward me. "Now let me see what those dreadful surgeons did to my star."

My eyes flicked toward Bernard in panic. He didn't so much as glance my way but took a step in front of me.

"Now is not a good time. Morgan just got back from the doctor's. She needs to lie down."

Cassandra stopped mid-stride, and her eyes flicked at me. "What's wrong? Why did she need to go to the doctor? And why am I just finding out about this now?"

Bernard took my arm and started leading me down the hall and into the bedroom.

"We just found out this morning, Cassandra. It's nothing major. She just has laryngitis. And I *did* tell you she wasn't feeling well, but you refused to believe me."

"Laryngitis!" Cassandra's clicking heels followed after us. "She can't have laryngitis, Bernard, she has to speak at the premiere in New York on Thursday."

I frowned up at Bernard, whose face gave nothing away. If he had known about going to a movie premiere, he certainly hadn't told me about it. The fact that he was avoiding eye contact made me believe he had to know about it and was merely biding his time before he sprang it on me.

"Well, you're going to have to reschedule it," Bernard said while ushering me into the bedroom.

"You want me to reschedule a movie premiere? What sort of power do you think I hold? She *has* to be there. She's the star of the goddamn film, Bernard! She is contracted to be there." Cassandra was waving her arms in the air, growing more hysterical as she spoke.

"The doctor says—"

"I don't give a rat's ass what the doctor says. Morgan is going to be at that premiere."

"She can't speak," Bernard hissed.

"Well, she can smile and wave. I can be there as her voice, but she will be there."

The last thing I wanted to do was go to a premiere, but it wasn't as though I could vocalize my objections with my made-up affliction. I had to rely on Bernard to save me.

"She needs to rest, Cassandra. That means you need to go."

Cassandra huffed. "I am not leaving until I talk to my client."

My eyes went to Bernard, who ignored her request and walked over to the bed and pulled back the covers, pointing at me to get in. Finding it potentially dangerous to my health to ignore him, I scrambled under the sheet and allowed him to tuck me in.

Bernard walked up to Cassandra, dwarfing her, definitely the more formidable of the two. "I'll give you five minutes.

Don't upset her. Remember, she can't make you any money if she gets worse."

Cassandra pursed her lips as Bernard brushed past her. He gave me one last look and left me alone with Morgan's scary ass agent.

Chapter 13

I lay in the bed, the covers drawn tight up under my chin, trying to hide as much of my body as possible, terrified she'd be able to tell I wasn't really Morgan. Cassandra paced the floor beside me. Her arms were crossed over her chest; her eyebrows were pinched tight, her red bottom lip stuck out in concentration. She was eyeing me with a level of suspicion that made me start to perspire. This wasn't going to work.

"There's something different about you," Cassandra purred. "No. Don't try to speak. We need to have you save that precious voice of yours for Thursday." Her eyes darted toward the closed door where Bernard had left just moments ago. "It's him, isn't it? He's the one you've been texting nonstop lately?" My eyes grew wide despite trying to stay neutral. "I *knew* it." She seemed dangerously calm. "I've seen the way he looks at you, but I never thought you'd become the cliché and do your bodyguard."

It would have been easy to let the matter drop, to let Cassandra believe whatever she wanted to about Bernard and Morgan. *I mean, really, what did it matter to me what she believed?* Except…I felt a twinge of protectiveness wash over me. I didn't want to be the one to reveal his secret crush. It seemed wrong. So, instead, I shook my head vehemently and gestured for something to write with.

Cassandra's eyebrow rose up in curiosity as she found a journal by my bedside and handed it to me.

I turned to a blank page and started scribbling. There was no forethought in what I wrote; I merely needed to take the spotlight off Bernard. I tore the page out and handed it to a waiting Cassandra who read it with perverted delight.

"Wait. Who is Scott? Was he your PA on *The Sun Will Rise Again*?" Cassandra made a face.

Again, I shook my head.

"So, who is he?"

I stuck my hand out for the paper, which she handed back as she sat on the bed waiting for her answer.

My head was spinning. I wasn't sure how much was safe to tell her, how much of this would get back to Scott, or how any of this would affect Morgan, but somehow I knew

Morgan would be more concerned if Bernard were thrown into the spotlight as her secret lover.

I wrote out the truth onto the page and handed it back to her.

"He lives here? A local? Jesus Christ, Morgan! Is that why you bought a place in the godawful town?" Cassandra blinked a few times.

I began writing again and explained that it was a schoolgirl crush. We'd met after I'd bought the place a few years ago and that nothing had come of it, and furthermore, Scott was gay anyway so it didn't even matter. The lies were mixing in with the truth so much that I felt myself flush from the embarrassing realization that I was falling for a man I couldn't have. Then again, what else was new? That tended to be the type of man I dated. I underlined twice that no one else knew.

Cassandra frowned. "You're damn right no one else will know. I will make sure of that." She stood up, tearing the pages into tiny pieces. "I know what you need. You need a man on your elbow at this premiere. It's been too long since you were seen with Kade. The media needs to have their super power couple again, especially after what you've done," she gestured with her arm in the direction of my face.

"I'm still furious with you for not telling me about this, by the way. I would have told you this was social suicide, but no, no one listens to their agents anymore." I opened my mouth, wanting to tell her where to go, but she held one manicured finger up at me. "No, you need to listen now. We have no time to sit and wait for this to die. You need to rise above this funk you're in and hold that new plastic head up high. You need to be seen at as many social functions as humanly possible. Your face needs to be plastered on every cover, not hiding away in some cabin in the woods. This is the new Morgan, proud and," Cassandra looked over at me, "I was going to say beautiful, but perhaps we should go with fresh?" The way she said it clearly indicated she agreed with the media coverage.

If Cassandra had any knowledge of Morgan's skin cancer, she would be singing quite a different tune, but again, it was not my place to say anything.

"Leave the salvaging of your image to me," she continued. "You just focus on getting better. I'll be in touch." With that, she rushed out of the room, a scheme clearly hatching in her mind and me being helpless to prevent it.

As soon as she left, I ripped off the covers and tiptoed to the door, waiting for her to leave. I heard her saying her goodbyes to Bernard, waited a few moments longer, and then came rushing out into the living quarters.

"What did you two talk about?" Bernard asked sternly.

I blew the hair out of my eyes, "You, actually."

That got his attention.

"Me? What about me?" He whispered, still aware of the cleaning crew lingering about. "Calm down. I fixed it. Everything is fine. Cassandra asked me if I, well if Morgan, was having an affair with you."

Bernard's entire face changed to one of unmasked horror. "What did you say? What did you tell Cassandra?" His arms had grabbed onto my shoulders, and he gave me a good shake.

"Nothing. I told her nothing," I said, pushing him off me.

Bernard stumbled back, as though composing himself. "I'm sorry, I just, have to protect Morgan from unwanted falsehoods."

"I know," I said, looking around to make sure the coast was clear. "But Cassandra suspected Morgan had a crush on someone, which is why I told her it was on Scott, not you." My face grimaced at the confession.

Bernard closed his eyes; he brought his hand to the bridge of his nose and pinched it several times before he spoke.

"You mean to tell me you told her about the guy with the cat?"

"I know! I know, it wasn't the smartest move, but it was the only thing I could think of at the time. Cassandra thought Morgan was texting you nonstop. Would you have rather me let her continue with that train of thought?"

Bernard walked over to the fireplace and rested both hands on the mantle as though trying to focus his mind. "What did she say to your confession?"

"She basically had the same reaction as you, to not let that tidbit of crushing on a gay man go public. Then she muttered something about getting me a date for the premiere on Thursday." A shiver ran down my spine at the thought of being out in public as Morgan. "Bernard, this isn't what I signed on for. I can't do this. I can't be a movie star. I'm not qualified. I am a temp, for God's sake. I don't know how to do anything but type and file papers. I can't walk down a red carpet with some hottie on my arm! I'll trip over my own feet. I'll say the wrong thing, I'll make a fool out of myself. Bernard, please don't make me do this."

I knew I was rambling, something I'd always done when I got panicked, but I was seriously starting to lose my shit. It was one thing to pretend to be a movie star in the safety of a closed-off mansion, quite another to rub elbows with other movie stars and pretend I actually knew what I was doing.

"Today's only Sunday. We have four days to get you ready. You're a quick learner. You must be, in your line of work." Bernard said with a tone of authority. "As a temp, you must be able to assess a job and mirror it in a proficient manner, yes?"

"I guess."

He nodded once. "Think of this as just another temp job. One that pays exceedingly well."

"A temp job?" I asked, considering him seriously. *Huh.* The entire gig was very much like a temp job if I thought about it. This too was a moment of time that I didn't need to live in forever. It wouldn't define me. I felt myself get calmer.

"Fine. Let's do this. But first, I need wine. Lots of wine."

Bernard cracked the faintest of smiles. "You got it."

As he strolled into the kitchen, I flopped down on the couch, where a curled-up Tripod slept.

"That looks like a great idea," I said, reaching my hand out to pet her fluffy head. My eyes closed in contentment. Who knew cats could melt away stress? "Maybe those crazy cat ladies are onto something." I sighed, as I lay back onto the couch next to Tripod, clinging to her warmth for a few blissful moments of serenity.

Chapter 14

During the course of the next several days, Bernard and I were like a clichéd film montage as we watched every red carpet, TV interview, and film Morgan had ever done. I needed to be prepared for what the press might ask me because I had no idea even what the movie was even about! Bernard assured me, however, that none of their questions would actually be about the film. He told me that female stars only get the superficial, airhead sort of questions, so I should be fine. I knew it was meant to comfort me, but I was offended for all womankind.

Unfortunately, as I watched more and more of the clips I saw that it was true; every single interview question we screened had to do with what Morgan was wearing or who she'd been seen dating. Her male counterparts, on the other hand, were asked in-depth questions about their performances and their choice of acting method. The women were treated as ornamental creatures at best.

"Oh, this is bullshit," I said after watching a TV interviewer ask Morgan to twirl in her gown. "Look at her! You can see how annoyed Morgan is that she's being asked to do this, but she doesn't say anything. She twirled! She actually twirled! Why doesn't she speak up?"

Bernard sighed softly, stood and turned the television off. "Trust me, she wants to. They all want to."

"Then, why don't they?"

"Because it's already hard enough for a woman in her thirties to land a role. You can't do anything to rock the boat. There is this unwritten law in Hollywood that from the ages of twenty-nine to fifty-nine, you're essentially un-castable." He shook his head in disgust. "Young ingénues and grandmas. That's all there is for women. It's as though Hollywood has completely forgotten about the stages of life in between."

I stood and started pacing, becoming irrationally enraged. Even though I had never paid much attention to it, he was right, roles for those of us in the middle part of their lives were few and far between and often portrayed by actors much younger than the characters they are meant to be playing.

Bernard must have seen my brow wrinkle with consternation because he approached and placed one giant hand on my shoulder. "This is not your battle. You will not say anything out of character for Morgan. Do you understand?"

I threw my hands up in the air. "Don't worry. I won't. But Morgan should. Someone should." I left the screening room disheartened and frustrated.

The days leading up to the premiere flew by too fast. My voice remarkably recovered and before I knew it, Cassandra called to say we'd be catching a flight to New York later that afternoon, and then I'd be rushed to the hotel where my hair and makeup team (I had a team, apparently) would descend upon me and get me *red carpet ready* for the night. There was a not enough Xanax in the world to prepare me for that.

I let out a breath. *Calm down, Jules, you just need to play the puppet for a little while longer. Then you can get back to the blessed seclusion of the mansion to ride out the rest of this wave.* Presuming the current one didn't kill me along the way.

As I flopped down face-first onto Morgan's bed, I heard Bernard's cell ring in the distance. His voice echoed off the walls. He sounded upset. Against my better judgment, I slid off the bed to eavesdrop at the bedroom door.

"Well, what are they saying?" I heard Bernard speak in a hushed, yet urgent tone. "But what about your white cell count? You said that was normal last week."

It had to be Morgan on the phone. I leaned out farther in the hall and could see Bernard's feet through the mini jungle of plants in the living room as he paced.

"Well, maybe they need to adjust the dosage if it's not working," he said, his voice wavering. "They need to do something, dammit. Do they have any idea who you are?" His voice rose for a moment, before turning quiet. "I know, I know. I'm sorry, I just—I should be there. I should be there with you."

Bernard's face came into view through the leaves. His hand was pressed over his eyes, head tilted to the floor, shoulders slumped. It seemed wrong to be witnessing his mental anguish. I eased myself back into the bedroom. I had heard more than I was supposed to and felt sick because of it.

Morgan wasn't doing well. Her last ditch effort was failing. It was a selfish thought to have. Where did that leave me? Where did that leave the lie? If she died, what then?

Needing to clear my head, I lost myself to the eight jet stream shower heads in the master bathroom. Not gonna lie, that was a perk I was going to miss.

When I finally emerged, I found a set of clothes had been laid out for me on the bed, with a note from Bernard. It read: *Put this on. Cassandra will be here in ten.*

"Excellent. Let the games begin."

For the last few days, Spanx had become a staple of my new wardrobe, just as Bernard had predicted. Although we looked alike in the face, in the hip area, I am vastly overqualified. I required multiple layers of fat-smoothing material in order to pull off the liquid coating of pants Bernard left for me. Apparently, breathing would be optional on this trip.

As I was pulling my hair into the messy side braid I'd seen Morgan wear on the cover of *Around Town* magazine, I noticed Bernard behind me in the reflection of the vanity mirror.

"You really *do* look like her," he said softly.

I turned around and gazed at him. "I'm sorry the treatment isn't working."

His eyes narrowed in question.

"I overheard you talking to Morgan earlier." His nostrils flared, and his posture straightened as though ready to go on the defensive. I reached out and took his hand. "Are you okay?"

Bernard stood frozen for a moment, but then I saw the careful mask he'd been wearing fall. He began to weep, the sort of cry that pours out from your body like an explosion. I stood on my tiptoes and took him in my arms, holding him as he sobbed into my shoulder. His emotions confirmed Morgan was not doing well, and the rock I had relied on during my own metamorphosis, the one I had found in Bernard, was now unable to keep my sanity afloat. It was my turn to hold him up.

"Well, well, well, what do we have here? Something going on between the two of you that you want to tell me about?" I opened my eyes as Bernard ripped himself off my shoulder and saw Cassandra standing there, her lips pursed in a knowing way.

Bernard was still struggling to pull his composure together, so I jumped to his aide.

"He's just had a death in the family, you nosy bitch," I said, feeling Bernard's shocked gaze fall on me. I had no idea if such a statement would be in character or not, but I went with it, brushing past her without acknowledgment. "I'll be in the car. Bernard, you can load the bags when you're ready. Take your time."

As I left the bedroom, I heard Cassandra fumbling to regain her composure, though Bernard said nothing to negate the lie I had told. Instead, he'd followed me outside to load the car.

Sinking into the leather seats, I rubbed my temples, trying to ward off the headache this trip was going to bring. When Cassandra finally joined me in the limo, she didn't speak. That suited me just fine. I opted to focus on the raindrops as they touched down on a gorgeous fall landscape. The colors were just now starting to pop. Specks of yellow and red kissed the edges of the trees giving them a color I'd never seen in the flesh. Although I had been here less than a week, I already felt homesick leaving the woods behind…even it was only going to be for a few days.

Chapter 15

Okay, I admit it. When Cassandra told me I would be flying out to New York, I assumed she meant in a big, normal, safe-looking plane. Wrong. Bernard drove the limo past the Manchester airport exits and headed to a different airport, coming to a stop only when we pulled into a lot for Private Jet Parking. Watching out the window, I saw a spattering of tiny-ass planes and nothing remotely resembling a plane big enough to carry people. Surely, these weren't real planes. These were the luggage planes. The people plane just wasn't there yet. That had to be it. When the limo stopped next to a jet that had ten windows total, my anxiety began to climb.

"What's wrong?" Cassandra asked.

I blinked a few times to regain my composure, forgetting for a moment, she was sitting beside me.

Bernard, once again, saved the day. "I tried to tell you she's still not a hundred percent. Just because her voice is back, doesn't mean she's fully recovered," he said in a smooth style. "There is some aspirin in your bag."

Through the rearview mirror, he gave me a knowing look that told me to do as instructed. I unzipped the bag and found, not aspirin, but a bottle of Valium instead. I quickly popped one, swallowing it down dry. I ignored the medicinal bite against the back of my throat as it passed my tongue. The foul taste would be worth it. I was going to need to remain calm to pull this thing off.

Bernard loaded our bags and boarded at the back of the plane leaving Cassandra and me all alone. I wanted the meds to kick in so I wouldn't have to be coherent for takeoff. That was the worst part. Well, that and the landing…and the whole flying in a death trap part.

Cassandra was on her phone typing madly before she tossed it onto the seat beside her, seemingly disgusted.

"I'm going to get some wine before we take off. Want anything?"

"No. Thanks."

She left me there. Alone. With her phone well within my reach. I could totally check my email real quick…just to see if Anthony had sent anything. I doubted he had. Still, my mind itched to know.

I glanced over the edge of the seat and saw Cassandra talking with Bernard, so I risked a quick look. Her phone was still unlocked, so I was able to navigate pretty quickly. I did my best not to see the texting conversation she was having with Kade Dermont about the premiere. The less I knew about that, the better.

A few minutes later, I was into my email account and scrolling past the messages from my mom and Macy. I prayed there would be a message from Anthony and also that there wouldn't.

I was just about to give up when a new message came in. My heart stopped. It was from Anthony.

You are being childish. Answer your phone or get your sexy ass over here. You know you can't resist me. I've watched you try and fail time and again. We're meant to be together, Jules. You know it, and I know it. She'll be at the gym at 5. Be here at 5:15.

The seatbelt sign came on just then, and I almost dropped the phone. Feeling oddly unclean, I quickly brought it back to the screen where Cassandra had been and tossed it onto the seat.

I didn't want to think about how right Anthony's statement was. How many times in the last three years had I tried to leave? How many times had he sucked me back in? Too many to admit even to myself.

Cassandra slid into the seat across from me just then and clicked her belt in place with a bored expression on her face, and a glass of white wine in her hand. She went right back to her phone as my eyelids began to droop. Valium made me sleepy, which was probably for the best. I was more than ready to forget about any thoughts for a moment.

"Honestly, Morgan. Pull yourself together," Cassandra said, waking me from my sleep. I checked out the view from the window. We had landed. I'd slept through the whole ride. Wonderful. "The paparazzi will likely be ready to pounce on you the minute you clear the gate," she said, pulling a case down from the overhead bin, "so the least you could do is wipe the drool off your face."

Bernard came up behind her and frowned at me as I wiped away the wetness with the back of my hand.

Cassandra left the plane allowing Bernard to hold out his hand to me. "Showtime," he whispered.

I nodded in understanding and put on my practiced Morgan pout. With large sunglasses in place, I almost felt as though this was just a game of dress-up, instead of the potentially career-ruining moment it could be.

Just as Cassandra had predicted, as soon as we walked out of the gate area, the paparazzi were there shouting Morgan's name. It was quite terrifying. At first, I couldn't make out what they were saying over the roar of voices, but then, one by one, the questions became clear.

"Was your plastic surgery done to keep you in the limelight?" one deep voice bellowed.

"What do your fans think about your new look?" came another.

"Were you pressured into the surgery?"

Bernard had forewarned me to pretend they weren't there by keeping my head down. He also told me not to trip. Always helpful that Bernard.

Flashes went off at a strobe-like intensity as the questions kept coming. It reminded me of a boxing match. Angry voices all trying to egg on the fighter into performing their best. The whole scene was also extremely disorientating. I couldn't see where to walk, let alone where the shouts were actually coming from.

Mercifully, Cassandra shadowed my left side, as Bernard guided my elbow on the right through the airport toward a waiting car.

"How does Kade Dermont feel about your dramatic change?" a woman shouted before we made it outside. She managed to get close enough to actually shove the microphone up to my face.

I glanced quickly at Bernard who merely shook his head once. I clenched my teeth and walked faster. Kade Dermont was uber famous. He had been listed as the Hunkiest Guy in America for two straight years. According to Bernard, Kade and Morgan had dated on and off, but currently, they were off. The way Bernard was avoiding glaring at me, however, confirmed he was a big fat liar. If Bernard expected me to try and be in the same room as a real life famous hunk, he was out of his mind. I would collapse in a heap on the floor and probably end up licking the actor's shoes instead. I was not to be trusted with a famous hottie.

After we got in the limo and pulled away, I let out a breath. "That sucked."

"Well, at least your surgery has kept you relevant. For now. Let's just hope it isn't also the thing that buries you," Cassandra said, pulling out her phone. Her fingers flew across the screen answering messages that must have come in during the flight.

I wanted to relax into the seat of limo but needed something answered STAT.

“Um, will Kade be at the premiere?” I asked as casually as possible. I saw Bernard’s eyes glare at me. *Please, say no, please, say no, please, say no.*

Without raising so much as an eyebrow from her phone, Cassandra scoffed. “Of course, he will, darling. He’s the date I arranged for you.” She focused on me and frowned. “Now, don’t start on me. I know you two aren’t together, officially, but both of you need the publicity. He’s been partying too hard for producers, and you need all the good press you can get now. Putting you two back together, at least in the eyes of the media, might just save both your careers.”

“Gee, thanks,” I said, a new wave of panic washing over me. I sensed Bernard trying to look at me, to communicate something, but I wouldn’t turn his direction. I was so far out of my element at the moment that I couldn’t breathe. I closed my eyes to try and stop the car from spinning.

I now understood why so many celebrities wore sunglasses, even at night; the rapid-fire flash of bulbs that greeted us when we got to the hotel was quite blinding. Tiny white dots burned holes in my retinas, dancing happily along the inside of my lids with each blink. It only seemed to cement the disorienting nature of this job.

Hoping against all odds, that once we reached the hotel room, I would be able to collapse in a heap and compose myself, I knew better. The second we entered the room, I was greeted by no less than a dozen people all seeming to talk at once. One woman dressed all in black with a band of quarter-sized pearls draped around her neck, and several garments draped over her shoulder, began holding up different dresses to me while another man ran fingers through my hair.

I tried really hard not to sink away from all of the unsolicited touching, but Bernard could see how uncomfortable I was becoming.

"Okay, people, let's give Morgan ten minutes, shall we? She's recovering from a pretty nasty cold, and I'm sure she would appreciate a few moments alone before you pounce on her."

Cassandra stared at Bernard with shock. "We only have four hours before the premiere."

"And now you only have three hours and fifty minutes. Go," Bernard said, pointing toward the door. Those in the room all glanced at one another.

I saw the challenge in Cassandra's eyes when she glared at Bernard. It was clear he didn't have the authority to make this call, but she was humoring him…for now.

She clucked her teeth and snapped her fingers, and they all left, one by one, out into the hall. When the door finally closed, I fell down, face first, onto the large white couch.

"Thank you," I said through the cushions.

"You have ten minutes to pull yourself together and remember who you are portraying."

When I heard the door close behind him, I rolled over and saw the chaos around the room; piles of clothes were heaped on racks along with shoes, hats, bags, and makeup. Holy Hannah, there was an entire coffee table covered with only cosmetics.

I rubbed away the headache that was forming at my temples as I tried to do a calming technique a former therapist had given me once. *Think of a happy place.* I let out a breath. A happy place. Right. *Where was I happy? In LA? With Anthony?* No. Definitely not happy then.

I rolled my shoulders. *Come on Jules…what makes you happy? If you could go anywhere right now, where would it be?* I figured I'd think of some remote desert island somewhere with a big cold piña colada, but instead, I found myself longing for the simplistic rental house back in New Hampshire, complete with its mass of unpacked containers and untapped potential. I longed to see the foliage that had just begun when I'd left to come here. I even missed Tripod. Me. Missing a damn cat. I found myself wondering if the maids were even feeding her the way I had instructed. I should have called Scott and had him pick her up early.

Scott.

Friday.

Shit.

Somehow, in the storm prepping for this premiere, I had completely forgotten about Scott coming on Friday to pick up Tripod.

As fast as I could, I scrambled off the couch and ripped open the door where I was greeted by a hallway full of people who were waiting impatiently for me to get my shit together. I found Cassandra's eyes instantly.

"When do we fly back?" I asked.

Cassandra pushed her way through the mass of bodies to reach me. "I have scheduled us leaving Saturday morning, Why?"

I shook my head vigorously. "No. We have to be back on Friday. By noon. I have a prior engagement that can't be rescheduled," I said with full authority. Now, realistically, I was sure there was a way to reach Scott and arrange for a later pickup, but I didn't want to do that. I wanted to see him. I needed to see another human who wasn't involved in the insane life I was currently living. I needed the sense of calm he brought.

"That's impossible. We have after-parties to attend on Thursday night. You'll be dead on your feet by Friday. Trust me. You will want to go back Saturday."

I shook my head vehemently. "We go back Friday, or we go back now."

Bernard cocked his head toward me but didn't say anything. I knew this was being incredibly selfish, but my sanity needed something to hold onto, something to make agreeing to do this whole charade worth it.

I'm not sure how I thought being friends with Scott was that foothold, but right now, it was what I was clinging to. I knew we could only be friends, but perhaps that's what I needed in my life. Learning how to be friends with a man I couldn't sleep with would be good for my soul. Maybe it would help me figure out what I really wanted in a guy. At the very least, he was pretty to look at.

At that moment, a timer went off on Cassandra's phone. My ten minutes were up.

"We'll talk about this later," she said as the crew of waiting workers rushed the door to get to me.

It didn't matter what they did to me now. I was able to zone the crew out as they began their work. I had found my happy place: daydreaming about that fugly couch in the rental, and staring longingly into a pair of unattainable, yet stunningly silver eyes.

Chapter 16

By the time they'd finished squishing my body into the gold sequin gown and cementing my hair down with spray in an attempt to make it look natural, I felt slightly molested. No less than five different pairs of hands had been on my ass and tits as they crammed every bit of fat into the dress. I lost count of the hairs that were ripped out of my head as they teased and smoothed it before they pinned it into the dramatic up-do. I didn't dare move for fear my neck would snap under the strain. For sure, it was gonna leave one killer headache.

"Okay, people, we have five minutes to get her into the car. Let's roll," Cassandra said, still glued to her phone. She lowered her head to me so only I could hear her. "Kade will be in the car so we can go over your stories before you walk the carpet."

I felt several hands on me as we left the room, each one trying to get in one last finishing touch to their masterpiece before they let me go.

"Our stories?" I asked, foolishly.

Cassandra walked with me while an entourage of people circled us as we approached the elevator where they continued to poke at me. I swatted one away like a fly.

"Honestly, Morgan it's as if you have forgotten everything about this business." She leaned in again. "You can't have conflicting stories."

I gaped at her, confused.

She sighed dramatically, and then with a snap of her fingers, she ordered the others away. I blinked at the power that one snap had. When they were out of earshot, she continued, "You'll have to come up with some reason why Kade was in Miami at that strip club while you are boarded up in the freaking mountains and sporting a brand new face." She made one of her own. "At this point, the only angle I can see is you changed your look in an attempt to make Kade love you," she said as she stared into the distance. "Hell, that would make a great TV movie. Hollywood actress goes under the knife to look more like the street trash her movie star boyfriend sleeps around with." She snorted before going back to her phone. “Obviously, that’s not the most flattering story for you, but unless the two of you come up with something better, that’s what we’re going with.”

My eyes searched for Bernard, hoping he would have some brilliant way to get me out of this upcoming conversation with a movie star, but the bodyguard was nowhere to be found.

Before I knew it, I was in the elevator, silently willing myself to disappear into the walls. This was my worst nightmare as an introvert, and I was about to live it in front of thousands of people, where it would be caught on film. Any failures would be preserved on the screen for all time.

The second the elevator doors opened, a flash of camera bulbs shocked me more than they should have. My skin started to crawl under the strobe of attention. I didn’t have sunglasses to hide behind. Without them, they would surely see the fear in my eyes, so I *had* to pretend. I had to show them I was stronger than I felt. Without a conscious thought, I found myself doing what I did each time Anthony told me he was leaving his wife. I raised my chin up high, locked a bright smile on my face and imagined everything was right in the world. It was a look I’d perfected over the years and was surprisingly easy to slip into.

The paparazzi went crazy at the uncharacteristic move because Morgan never smiled in public. Never showed any emotion except those damn duck lips, but at that moment, I needed *my* strength not hers.

Cassandra's arm pulled me forward through the cameras and out through large golden lobby doors where a whole new crew of cameras had set up. Naturally. Although my cheeks were starting to burn while holding the smile in place, I kept it up. Only a few more seconds and I'd be in the limo, safe from the watchful eye of the media. So far so good. Maybe I could pull this off after all?

Just then the back door of the car waiting for us opened, and out stepped Kade-f'ing-McDermot in the hotter-than-hell flesh.

The paparazzi lost their shit as they turned their lenses toward him, each pushing the other to vie for the perfect shot.

Kade was dressed head-to-toe in a spotless white tux, his ebony skin glowed against the backdrop of the matching white limo behind him. He flashed his famous half-grin, much to the delight of the photographers around him before he turned to look at me.

OMG. Kade McDermot was walking towards me!

His six foot two gait reached me in three quick strides. I only had enough time to open my mouth in astonishment at his movie star presence before he pulled me into an embrace and crammed his tongue down my throat…like touching my tonsils sort of tongue.

Now, one might think being molested by a movie star would be every girl's ultimate fantasy. Hell, even I had daydreamed about this man's lips on mine more than once. But at that moment, all I wanted to do was bring my knee up into his nether regions and drop him down to the ground for his ballsy move. The frantic clicking of cameras going off around us kept me grounded in reality. I needed to keep my cool because we were being watched. Oh, how we were being watched.

When Kade finally came up for air, the paparazzi began shouting even more fervently than before. I couldn't make out a single word, however. It all sounded like one giant swelling roar. Kade seemed to eat it up. He wrapped his hand around my waist and locked me to his side as he waved to the crowd.

In a moment, another pair of hands pushed us toward the car. A quick glance behind me confirmed it was Bernard. Finally, a friendly face.

All four of us were in the car a few seconds later, and the limo pulled us away from the circus, and I let out a breath.

"Damn, girl, what the hell did you do to your face?" Kade asked, frowning. "I knew you were going to look different, but you're like a whole other person. If it hadn't been for that kiss, I would have never recognized you."

I glared at him hoping the small smirk creeping onto my lips wouldn't give away the irony.

"Way to be a jackass, Kade," Cassandra said, taking the words out of my mouth. "It is none of your business what my client does to her face. What does concern me is the stunt you just pulled back there. You and I both know you don't care about Morgan and would rather be in a hotel room with some cheap skank, so please don't drag her into your pathetic publicity stunt in some feeble attempt to improve your image."

My mouth dropped. This was the first time Cassandra had ever stood up for me. *Well, stood up for Morgan, that is.*

Kade's expression was one of bemused interest.

"Cut the crap, Cassandra. Both of our images will be improved if we're seen together. It worked last time and the time before that." Kade reached over and grabbed my knee and shook it gently. "We are each other's toxic cleansing.

People love us together. There's no harm in giving them a show as long as they give us the press we want. You, of all people, should know that." He leaned back in the limo, tipped his hat up and closed his eyes.

Cassandra's normal powder-white skin began to rage with crimson. The color started at her neck and clawed its way into her cheeks, filling like a thermometer about to burst. I inched back into my seat, not wanting to catch any heat from her building anger.

"So that's it? You're just going to kiss my client whenever you want?" Cassandra practically squealed. I cocked my head. Shrieking was not something I gathered Cassandra did often. She was flipping out too hard over a publicity stunt. A stunt she probably would have suggested herself at some point. I didn't understand why she was getting so upset over a stupid kiss.

A kiss.

My eyes darted back and forth between Kade and Cassandra. She was fuming. Angry that he had kissed me. This wasn't a simple case of an agent being angry that her client was being manipulated. This was jealousy, and I had become the unwilling center of it all.

Kade opened one eye. "Girl, you know I always look out for number one. Now shut the hell up. I'm still coming down from my bender, and that kiss got me all worked up." He made a blatant move to adjust his pants.

I made a face that could only be described as disgust as he closed his eyes again, wearing a smile that indicated he was pleased by my reaction. Kade stretched out his long legs to settle in for the ride to the red carpet, ignoring us both.

My stomach churned. My image of Kade McDermot was shattered. He wasn't the sultry yet nice guy he played in his movies. He was a two-faced asshole. He showed the press his good side, and we got stuck with the backside. Was I any different, though? Wasn't I leading a double life too?

I wrapped both arms around my waist as though to hold on tight to the real me in all this madness. I had to remember who I was. This night wasn't me. This life I was living wasn't mine. Then why did the pain of it feel so real?

Chapter 17

The tension against my head only managed to mount as the limo got in line with others to drop us off. There were literally dozens of them, just like ours, patiently awaiting proper delivery times at the red carpet. It would take all of sixty seconds to get out of the car from where we were and just walk to where we needed to be, but no, there was a protocol to follow. A car pulled up, famous people attending the movie would get out, have their pictures taken, and walk down the line of waiting reporters. As the star of the film, I was to be dropped off last, giving me ample time to worry.

I tried to hide my anxiety from Cassandra, who was still clearly upset. Her body language was angled away from Kade, and she only glanced at me when speaking to both of us.

“Remember, when you get out, just smile and wave. Kade, keep your hands off my client,” she warned Kade before turning back to me. "I will direct you to which reporters are worthy of our time."

I nodded as if I knew what she meant. Bernard had coached me about the sorts of questions likely to be asked, and I had my rehearsed sound bites at the ready. This was going to be twenty minutes of my life. Tops. That reminder didn't make me feel any better.

Cassandra glanced out the window, seeming to calculate our arrival time. "Remember to keep your answers brief and to the point."

Kade lifted his head off the chair and sat up. "Yes, Mom."

I saw Cassandra's jaw tense for a split second, but she never acknowledged him.

"Once you get inside, look for your place card. It will be up front, but the usher will escort you. After the film, we have a string of after-parties—"

"Um, I already told you. I'm not going to those. I have to get back."

Cassandra glared at me. "Don't be ridiculous. You *will* go. You are the only reason they're having the parties. This is promotion time. If you don't show up to every event, your movie will tank. You do not want to piss off these people. They are your bread and butter."

I wanted to tell her I didn't give a rat's ass about any of this but I held my tongue. I wasn't exactly sure how I was going to get to New Hampshire tomorrow, but I was going to get there, with or without Cassandra's permission.

The night passed in a whirlwind of fake smiles, weak handshakes, and limp congratulations. I vaguely remembered answering the predictable questions posed by the reporters lined up out front. Cassandra seemed to know instinctively which reporters would stick to their script, and which ones would ask me personal questions about my face, or about Kade. I might as well have been on a leash as my wrist was yanked from microphone to microphone. My eyes were blurry from all of the flashbulbs, and my head was killing from the up-do, so by the time the movie began, all I wanted to do was sneak out back and escape the madness.

I probably should have. The after-parties were just as clichéd and ridiculous as every place I'd seen them depicted. People were snorting coke while attractive blondes clung to the sides of clearly rich and influential older men. Everyone else was brown-nosing somebody trying to get a leg up. I had never been more uncomfortable in my entire life, and yet, I should have felt right at home. Everyone was pretending to be someone they weren't, just like me.

Kade didn't help matters. All night long, his hands were on my waist or my ass, no matter how many times I subtly removed them. When two in the morning rolled around, I had more than enough. I had done my part. I had satisfied my obligations. I wanted to go home.

Still standing at Kade's side while he was talking to some big-boobed brunette about her latest porn film, I excused myself. Knowing he would be fully engaged in that conversation for a long time, I used it as my opportunity to escape. Bernard had given me some petty cash before we left so I could easily hail a cab and catch a train or something. Unlike Morgan, I knew how to move around in the real world. I didn't need every part of my life micromanaged.

As I checked down the street for a taxi, I heard footsteps approach from behind.

"Leaving so soon?"

I turned around to see Bernard standing there, a knowing grin on his face. There would be no point in lying to him. He'd be able to spot it.

"I need to get back. The kitten. Scott. I told him I'd meet him at noon on Friday." I frowned. "Well, today."

Bernard's eyebrows raised slightly. "*That* was your prior engagement?"

I lowered my head to the ground. "You have your priorities. I have mine."

"Well then, let's get you home." Bernard turned and gestured to our limo. As much as I wanted nothing more than to disappear into that car, I hesitated.

"Cassandra will be pissed if you help me."

"I don't work for her. I work for you. If you want to leave, I make that happen. Besides, I'm Scott's lift to the mansion, am I not?" He gave me a quick wink and nodded toward the car.

Satisfied, I climbed into the limo to let Bernard carry out my escape plan.

"Now, we have one of two options. We head to JFK and risk being seen—or worse, not able to get a direct flight—or we can drive straight on through," Bernard asked from behind the wheel.

"Drive? How long would that take?"

Bernard shrugged. "Traffic would be light, probably four and a half hours, tops."

"Could you stay awake that long?" A yawn rocketed through me. "It's really late."

He grinned. “I slept through the movie. I’m all rested up.”

I stuck my tongue out at him, jealous that he got to catch a few winks and I didn’t. The thought of being able to close my eyes for a few hours during the drive was more tempting than I could refuse. “To the open road then,” I said, letting out another yawn.

He laughed and wished me good night before he rolled up the privacy window and pulled out of the parking spot.

“I’m coming home, Tripod. I’m coming home.” I curled up against the seats and drifted off to the thoughts of orange fur against my nose and the promise of someone with silver eyes knocking on my door. No. *Stop it Jules. Stop it right now*. Scott is only a friend. A friend. Don’t turn into one of those girls who falls in love with a gay man. Just don’t do it. *Don’t you dare become obsessed with yet another man you can’t have!*

Rolling over, I felt a few bobby pins poking into my brain, so I yanked them out of my hair before finally succumbing to the gentle rock of the car and into pull of sleep.

I awoke to the sound of what I thought were car doors slamming. The crunch of gravel indicated several brisk, short strides. I opened one eye and saw the early morning sky against a stationary background. We had stopped. Sitting up, I was surprised we were home already. The car was in the driveway. Bernard was gone.

As I tried to get my bearings, I massaged a kink out of my neck. My head throbbed from not enough sleep, the noise and smoke from the parties and the concrete blob still semi-attached to my head. I began ripping out the rest of bobby pins to relieve some of the pain when I noticed movement out of the corner of my eye. The servants were arriving for the day. They came in a small white van as a team. From seven in the morning to seven in the evening, a rotation of five servants came and went. They had it down to a science.

Watching the group from the lingering warmth of the limo, I fished out the last pin. I groaned, feeling my hair limp its way back down my neck.

From where I sat, I watched Bernard open the door and say something quiet to them from near the doorframe. A moment later, the bewildered crew shuffled back to their van and drove out of the driveway as he went back inside. Bernard watched them leave then quickly went back inside. Curious, I got out of the car and made my way inside.

The house was unusually warm and appeared to have every light turned off. Even the sun wasn't bright enough yet to properly illuminate the room, so I flicked on the switch as soon as I got inside.

"What are you doing? Turn off that light!" Bernard hissed at me.

"Why? It's dark in here." I kicked off my heels and tossed my purse on the counter with a loud thunk.

"Will you keep it down?"

I blinked a few times trying to understand what was going on. "Why do I need to be quiet? And why did you send the staff away?"

"I fired them. Be quiet."

"If you expect me to do the chores too while I'm here, you are hired the wrong chick, buddy," I said massaging my foot.

Bernard's nostrils flared, but he didn't speak. Instead, he pointed at the fireplace, or rather, more specifically, to the blob sitting next to the fire. I squinted to make out what it was…and gasped.

"Morgan?"

"In the flesh," she croaked.

Holy shit.

Chapter 18

I'm not sure how long I stood there with my mouth open. Morgan Malone, the *real one,* was in the same room with me. I shouldn't have been star struck, considering my role in all of this, but there I was, my mouth ajar, with no clue what to say.

"But…how…why…" I blurted out. *Smooth, Jules. Real smooth.*

Bernard took a few steps closer and escorted me into the kitchen.

"I'm just as surprised as you are," he whispered. "I walked in here and found her there by the fire. She's got a fever and can't stop shaking." The crease in his eyebrows gave away his true concern over the situation. "She wore a black wig and sunglasses and had a cabbie drop her off a few blocks away. She walked here during nightfall so the paparazzi wouldn't find her. In that condition!" He looked back over at her for a moment as though he hated the fact he wasn't snuggled beside her.

"She's on the last round of the medicine." His eyes welled up. He lowered his voice even softer, so I had to strain to hear him. "She didn't want to be alone if…if it failed."

"Jesus," I whispered.

"I already tried him, kid. He is not taking my calls."

Morgan brushed by the two of us just then, without even looking at me, Tripod in one hand, her other gripping the edge of an oversized comforter, cocooning her frail body beneath. As the kitten climbed onto her shoulders, batting playfully at the loose threads of the blanket, Morgan opened the fridge door, grabbed a bottle of wine, dug inside a drawer for a bottle opener and hugged them both to her chest. She ignored us both as she passed both of us to plop back down onto the couch.

Bernard and I looked at each other for a moment but then followed after Morgan, sitting beside her and gently rubbing her back.

"Should you be drinking?" Bernard asked, checking the labels of the assortment of bottles beside her for alcohol warnings.

"Lay off, Bernard," I heard myself saying. "Let the woman have a drink." I grabbed a glass from a nearby wine rack and brought it over to her.

Morgan's gaze raised up at me, accompanied by a weak smile.

"Yeah. What she said."

Morgan struggled with the bottle for a moment longer before Bernard took over, opened it and poured her a hearty glass.

After she had taken a large swig, she collapsed back into the couch and closed her eyes. Morgan looked like shit. Her cheeks had hollowed; the color of her skin was ashen. She likely hadn't slept in days. Her hair fell lifeless and unstyled around her shoulders. Gone was the glamor girl I'd studied and in her place was a woman who looked more like me on a normal day. That, in itself, was disturbing.

Not knowing what I should do, I turned to Bernard for guidance, but he only had eyes for Morgan. It was clear how much he cared for her and she for him. I found myself irrationally jealous of their bond.

"I'll just leave you two alone," I said.

Neither of them said anything when I got up. Morgan's eyes remained focused on the fire in front of her while Bernard's attention locked in on her vacant expression, as though waiting for a flash of the woman he knew to return to him.

My first thought was to go to my room, but I realized it wasn't really my room. Nothing here was mine. Once again, I found myself without a place to call home.

I didn't have the heart to ask Bernard for the keys to the limo, so instead, I decided to go outside. Maybe walk around the grounds or something.

Before I left, I snagged my sunglasses and an off-white throw that was draped over the edge of the wingback chair and wrapped it around my shoulders before heading outside. This would have to be my disguise, though I really didn't think any paparazzi were lurking around. Sometimes, I swore it was just Bernard's way of keeping an eye on me.

There were plenty of places along the property to sit and wait for the shit-storm inside to blow over. Unfortunately, none of them seemed right. I was an intruder in someone else's life. I didn't belong here.

The real Morgan was back, which meant there was no place for me now. No place in LA either. All of a sudden, I started to feel incredibly lonely.

Normally, whenever I got like this, I'd call Macy, and we'd go out to a few bars and get drunk, and everything would be right with the world. But I couldn't call her. I couldn't go out with the girls to blow off steam. I had no contact with anyone from my past. At least, until the plan was over. Maybe that time was now. I wasn't sure. I didn't know what was happening, so I just walked.

My head was spinning. Nothing felt right anymore. I craved my life before all this fame crap started. Back when I was at the rental house. I saw myself there, sitting on the worn floorboards of the stairs, watching the leaves fall. I visualized having a moment of Zen or some bullshit. I needed to refocus. Regroup.

I had a plan. I'd go there. Get my head on straight. Then I could come back and face whatever reality was waiting for me back at the mansion.

My feet found their way back to the rental far easier than I would have imagined. It was like finding my way back home.

I was smiling when I crested the hill, eager to get inside and flop onto the couch. My smile disappeared, however, when I spotted a pickup truck loaded with stuff in the driveway. I felt my heart dip. *Had the place already been re-rented?*

Just then, I noticed a middle-aged man carrying a dark blue suitcase with a bag tag in the shape of a high heel shoe dangling from its corner. That was *my* bag. Macy had given me that bag tag. The tears melted away and evaporated into anger.

Without thinking, I marched forward and shoved the man, hard.

“Hey! That’s mine!”

The heavyset man turned and studied me. He was two times larger than me, but I didn’t falter in my stance. His eyebrows had pinched in confusion before he glanced up at the teenager who had been organizing items in the back of the truck. The boy just shrugged his shoulders.

Narrowing my eyes, I took a closer look at what was inside the truck and noticed the items inside it were all mine.

“What the hell? This is my stuff. What are you doing with all of my stuff?”

The teenager made a face. “Um, we’re moving it.”

“Yes, I can see that. Why are you moving it?”

“Because we were hired to.” A third voice answered from behind me. A voice I instantly recognized. I spun around and saw him standing there, tattered jeans, dark red plaid shirt dangled over a fitted grey T-shirt. A blue baseball hat covered his curls. He looked sexy as hell. It was as though God was taunting me with something I couldn’t have. All the more reason to become an atheist.

"Scott," I stammered, feeling the blush creep into my cheeks. "What's going on?"

"Why don't you guys take five?" Scott nodded toward the house. The older gentleman held out a hand for the teen to jump down and the two of them disappeared into the rental.

"What is going on?" I asked again, taking off my sunglasses.

Scott jumped up onto the back of the tailgate and patted the metal truck bed beside him, offering me a seat.

"I think I'll stand if you don't mind."

Scott smirked for a fraction of a second but nodded in understanding.

"You were telling me why you were touching my stuff…"

He chuckled. Dammit all if it wasn't adorable.

"I already told you. We were hired to."

I crossed both arms over my chest, trying to seem as stern as someone draped in a cashmere throw can look.

"Are you trying to tell me someone hired a pediatric nurse to move my unmentionables?" I nodded toward my suitcase.

"No. He hired a moving company."

It was my turn to make a face.

"He? Explain."

Scott tapped the edge of the tailgate again as a clear condition of obtaining the truth. Frowning, I obliged him and wiggled my fat ass onto the edge of the truck.

"I don't *live* at the hospital, you know. I do have free time. And when I do, I sometimes help out Allen. That would be the guy you accused of stealing your suitcase."

"Wait. Are you trying to tell me that you save babies' lives full-time *and* move people's furniture on your day off, for fun?"

He laughed softly. "I know. It's not a very logical pairing, but it's a way to give back to my community. Allen is also a janitor at the hospital, and he runs this company on the side but can't afford a lot of help, so I pitch in from time to time. That's all." He shrugged. "There are lots of jobs I've done over the years. I've been a waiter, worked at the auto shop for a few weeks, helped out at the schools for a month, the CPR training you saw. Hell, I was even a garbage man for a time." He shivered at the memory before twisting over his shoulder at me, noticing my confusion.

"Was this before you became a nurse?"

Shaking his head, he smiled. "No, this was all in the last few years, I guess."

I made a face. “Man, I thought nurses made better money than that. I hate working one job, let alone two.”

He rubbed his hands together a few times. “It’s not just about the money. I am saving up to maybe go back to school one day, but it’s more than that, too…it’s just—” He was having a really hard time trying to explain himself. “I find that I am able to connect more with the parents of my patients if I’ve been able to walk in their shoes, at least for a while. One way I can do that is to work the jobs they work. It helps me understand the hardships they face, but also the joy. It teaches me compassion.”

I sat there for a minute, too stunned to speak.

“I know it seems foolish for a nurse to care so much about their patients, but I do. I’m a bit of a sap, I suppose.”

“No, that’s pretty cool. I don’t think I could ever do that.”

Scott smiled. “It’s not that hard. After all, they’re only temp jobs. Just a small taste of their lives.”

I nodded. “Yeah, I work temp jobs. They’re great.” My eyes widened as I realize what I just confessed about my true self. “By that I mean…each acting gig is temporary. Pretending to be someone else for a bit,” I quickly recovered, hoping I sounded convincing.

"I can see that," Scott said. "See? We're not so different, you and I." God, his eyes were intense.

"So, um," I said, shaking my head away from his gaze. "Where are you taking my stuff?" I could only assume this 'He' had been referring to was Bernard. He had said he'd take care of the rental. I guess this was how it was being handled.

"We're taking it to a storage unit for you. I was thinking I could drop off the key to you later this afternoon when I come pick up Tripod." There was something in the way his eyes looked at me that seemed an awful lot like hope. Or I was just plain misunderstanding his body language. I was really good at that.

"Yeah, about that…" I said. He couldn't come to the house. With Morgan back, I couldn't risk him seeing her, but at the same time, I didn't want to give up that meeting either.

Scott hopped off the bed of the truck.

"I knew it," he said, shaking his head.

"You knew what?"

He turned and walked over to me. His body dangerously close between my legs as they dangled off the truck bed.

"You've fallen in love."

My mouth went dry. My face burned twelve shades of scarlet. *Holy shit…did he just call out my crush on him?* My mouth hung open.

"You, the girl who said she hated cats, has fallen helplessly in love with Tripod." Scott smirked.

I let out a huge breath…a mix of relief and sorrow, if I was honest.

"You got me. What can I say? The little shithead has grown on me."

There was no mistaking his next move. Scott took an intentional step forward, placing his hips directly between my thighs. I began to sweat. His face was mere inches from mine. I may suck at reading people, but there was no way to confuse this with something else. Even my heart was racing. He started to lean in. *Holy shit!* He was going to kiss me! Why?

"But," I whispered, "You're gay…"

He pulled his head back and cocked it to the side, clearly amused. "I am?"

"I mean, aren't you? Isn't Liam your—"

His hands cupped the sides of my face and brought my eyes up to his.

"Liam is one of the nurses I work with and as flaming as they come, but he is only a friend." His thumb traced my bottom lip ever so slowly as he spoke again. "I am one hundred percent heterosexual."

I gasped. "You mean—" I swallowed hard.

He inched even closer. "I like women. I like you."

"Oh," I whispered.

He started to lean in again but stopped, a breath away. His husky voice came hot in my ear.

"May I kiss you, Morgan?"

It took me a second to remember he was talking to me.

"Um…yes, please." I panted. Yes, I actually panted.

He pulled back to look at me as though a thought popped into his head. "You're not spoken for then?" His eyes pierced mine, searching for the right answer.

"Spoken for? Me? God, no. I'm not seeing anyone."

A smile danced on his lips.

"Well, in that case…"

His face lowered to mine and in the middle of a crisp autumn day, with golden leaves dancing delicately around us, I had my first-ever body tingling, borderline erotic kiss. Even in the throes of the not suitable for TV make-out session, I knew it was a matter of time before I screwed this up. But for now, I was going to relish each and every delicious moment.

Chapter 19

The kiss came to an abrupt halt when a low whistle was heard from the porch. We pulled apart from each other like school children caught by our parents to discover the teenager grinning knowingly at Scott.

"Way to go, Mr. Jacobs," the kid shouted. "making out with a movie star!"

Scott closed his eyes in embarrassment. "Would you mind giving us another second, Justin?"

The kid smiled even wider. "Sure thing." He hovered for a second longer though before going back inside.

"Well, that wasn't at all mortifying," I said, hopping off the tailgate. I crammed hands into my pockets and focused on the ground, fully aware of how red my cheeks were.

"Don't mind him. He's just a horny kid," Scott said with a wicked grin.

"Yeah, well, even so, I should probably go," I said, hitching behind me toward the road.

"Where's your bodyguard?"

"That's why I need to go. Bernard doesn't know I left." I made a face. "I just needed some time to think, you know?"

"Well," Scott said as he lifted his arms upward, "the scenery here does lend itself to deep thoughts."

I nodded slowly. "You may be right. When I left the mansion, I had no idea where I was going. My feet sort of ended up here. I'm not sure why."

Scott took a step toward me, grabbed both ends of the throw around my shoulders and held me there for a moment. "I know why. The universe wanted us to meet again. It keeps finding ways to bring us together." His eyes froze on mine, no trace of humor rested there.

"You mean to tell me you believe in all that fate mumbo-jumbo?"

He smirked. "You'd be surprised about what I believe."

I laughed despite the truth that quite possibly lived there.

"Perhaps, one day, I'll find out," I said off the cuff, but really wanted it to be true.

"Perhaps you will." He reached up and grabbed my chin lightly. "And maybe, one day you'll share some of your truths, too?"

I pulled my chin out of his grasp faster than I probably should have. “What’s that supposed to mean?”

He shrugged. “I can tell you’re hiding something from me.” I tried to protest, but he held up his hand. “I’m not saying you need to tell me anything right now, but maybe one day, you’ll trust me with whatever secret that’s eating at you.”

This was going down a dangerous road, so I needed to change the subject. “I really should be getting back. Bernard might call out the Brute Squad once he realizes I’m not really taking a bath.” I tried to pull away from Scott, but he held the throw still draped over my shoulders firmly in his hands.

“Not so fast,” he purred. He was looking down at me, his eyes intent on my lips. “I believe you still owe me something.” His eyes locked with mine. My body tingled at the insinuation. He wanted a goodbye kiss, the greedy little bugger. My face reddened, and I bit my bottom lip, insanely turned on at his request, but I willingly placed my lips on his. The kiss was soft and gentle this time, yet still tinged with desire. It was the sort of embrace I always hoped I would get from Anthony…hell, from all of my past boyfriends. Hollywood promised those kinds of kisses. I didn’t believe they were real, until now.

Macy had told me that one day I'd be locked in a full body *zing* and when I felt that, he was the one I needed to marry.

I stepped away from him, trying to get a grip on all of the thoughts running rampant in my head.

"That was nice," Scott said, "but a kiss was not what I was talking about."

My face contorted in puzzlement. Was he insinuating something else? Something beyond a kiss? My heart sank. Was he really like every other guy and only interested in sex?

"Get your mind out of the gutter," Scott scolded playfully. "I'm talking about Tripod. I believe you still owe me a kitten. Noon still work to pick her up?"

"Oh, right, that." This, after the lengths I went to in order to get back here in time for his visit. "Well, it turns out today isn't a great day, after all." I wasn't quite sure what to tell him. While I couldn't risk blowing Morgan's cover, it seemed so wrong to lie to him. Instead, I told as much of the truth as possible. "I have a friend at the house who's sick."

Scott's eyebrows shot up into the air.

"A friend?" The jealousy on his face was clear and ridiculously attractive.

"A female friend," I clarified. His face softened. "She's not well and needed a place to chill for a while. I offered her my couch."

"You're a good friend."

I shrugged. "Some friend. Here I am talking to you instead of helping to take care of her." Even though I barely knew Morgan, it did feel a bit childish to walk out on her. Sure, I told myself it was so she and Bernard could have time to talk, but the truth of the matter was I didn't do well with sick people. Guilt crept in. "I went for a walk because I got scared. She's really sick, like the sort of sick she might not bounce back from. I don't know what to do. I don't know what to say."

Scott nodded and rubbed the pad of his thumb on my shoulder. "In my line of work, I have to deal with a lot of illness. Babies who are given odds that are grim at best, some moms who have hemorrhaged so badly and are given no hope at all." His eyes lowered as though remembering the losses. "There is a lot of fear around those who are sick or dying, a lot of uncertainty. One thing that *is* predictable, though, is that once that bad news comes in, their visitors disappear. People who they thought cared the most, begin to vanish from their lives simply because they don't know what to say. They don't know how to help, so they do nothing." He focused off into the distance, but I could see his eyes had glazed over. How many deaths had he been witness to in his job? How much heartbreak had he lived through? "Illness is terribly lonely for far too many. But it doesn't have to be. You don't need to know the right words to say, Morgan. You just have to *be there* for her to hear them."

My throat thickened at the honesty. It made perfect sense. That was why Morgan had came back, after all. If she was going to die, she was going to do it in her own home and by the side of someone who loved her. She didn't want to go it alone.

"Why don't you let me drive you back so you can be with her?" he asked nodding toward his truck that was parked on the side of the road.

"No, I couldn't ask you to do that."

"You didn't ask. I offered." He gave me a gentle smile.

I shook my head. "I don't think she'll be up for meeting new people. She's kind of weak. Embarrassed about how she looks…" That last one I knew was true. She was horrified that she mirrored me, a mere commoner.

“I won’t go in. I’ll just drive you to the door. Okay?” His big eyes looked up at me like a wounded puppy. How could I say no to that face? Like for any reason, ever?

“Oh, fine. Just to the driveway, though.”

I waited as Scott ran into the house to let the movers know he would be back shortly. We walked over to his truck that was parked across the street. He opened the passenger side door for me, and I blushed again.

“Wow, you open doors, too?”

“Chivalry is not dead, my Lady.”

I took his proffered hand and jumped up into the truck.

“Why thank you, my Liege.”

He laughed and walked around the front of the truck and got in. A moment later, the engine roared to life.

“I don’t think I’ve ever been in a truck before,” I said, fastening my seatbelt. “Is that weird?”

Scott pulled out onto the road and glanced over at me.

“They don’t have trucks in LA?”

“I’m sure they do, just none of my friends do. Most of the cars out there are tiny, fuel-efficient matchboxes. Something like this would kill a fuel budget.”

He nodded as he pulled out onto the road. “You lived in LA your whole life, then?”

I leaned over and rested my head against the doorframe. "Mostly. A wasted life, as it turns out."

"Wasted?"

I let out a breath. "It doesn't matter. It's in the past. I came out here for a fresh start." I wasn't about to tell him about Anthony. Not because it would be against my contract, but because I was ashamed of it.

"Got it. You don't want to talk," he said, turning on the radio.

"About my past, no. I don't. Sorry."

Scott nodded once. "That's okay. I don't care to talk about my past much either. No point in looking back, right?"

"Exactly."

We drove the rest of the way listening to some crazy show about car repairs on public radio. The guy's laughs were infectious. It was quite refreshing not be forced into small talk. Anthony hated the radio and silence so it was up to me to come up with clever things his wife wouldn't.

It was quite nice just sitting beside a man without the pressure to be *on*.

When he pulled the truck up the spiraling drive, I didn't want the moment to be over. Our time together had been so relaxed. When we crested the hill of Morgan's house, Scott let out a whistle.

"Nice place you got here."

The reality of who I was, or who I was pretending to be, came crashing in. He was crushing on a movie star. *Not me*. I had to remember that.

"Um, thanks," I said, looking up ahead, a bit distracted by a bunch of cars and vans that shouldn't be there. A cluster of people were shouting at each other in a circle. I couldn't make out who they were, though I suspected paparazzi. *Oh, God, had they discovered the truth? Was Morgan's cover blown?*

Chapter 20

I was out of Scott's truck before the wheels had even come to a full stop. The loud squeal of the door's metal hinges betrayed my sneak attack, but it didn't matter. I had precious few seconds to find out who these people were and why they were outside Morgan's house.

"What's going on?" I shouted over the overlapping conversations. The crowd of people broke apart enough for me to see Cassandra standing in the center of the vultures. The look of relief at seeing me was beyond evident.

"Morgan!" she exclaimed. She lifted her hand and gestured toward me. "See? She is not sick in bed. She is standing right here. Whoever your source was who claimed they saw Morgan entering this house earlier was clearly mistaken." Cassandra wore a satisfied, yet thoroughly frustrated smile. From the short time I'd known her, I realized she was the type who didn't like being left out of the loop. Clearly, she had no idea what was really going on, but she seemed thrilled that, in this instance, the media had it wrong. Little did she know they had actually hit the nail right on the head.

The cameras turned then and started snapping pictures with their bright flashes, causing me to squint against their assault…always a good look for the tabloid covers. All at once, a surge of voices rose as they barked out asinine questions.

"Who was that who went into your house earlier?"

"Why did you leave New York in such a hurry?"

"Did Kade hook-up with that pole dancer in Florida?"

"What are you trying to cover up?"

I refused to answer their asinine questions. I didn't need media training to understand when I was being manipulated into saying something wrong or having my words taken out of context.

"This is private property. I want you all to leave, or I'll call the cops."

"Why are the curtains drawn in your house?"

My nostrils flared. I spun around and looked dead into the eyes of the busybody female reporter who looked back at me with wide eyes for a moment. She held her microphone up higher to capture my rage.

"Gee, I wonder why I'd want to close my blinds? Because looking out at scum like you doesn't interest me."

The reporter didn't bat an eye. "My source says a woman entered your property alone and had a key. She looked an awful lot like you. How do you explain that?"

"How do I explain that I have a house guest who's blonde and tall? I would guess her parents' DNA had something to do with that."

More flashbulbs. I cursed myself. I was feeding their frenzy and had let them see me get angry. It was clear. However, they weren't going to leave until they got a story. Fine. I'd give them one.

"You wanna know who I have in there? It's my friend. She's dying from cancer, you sick turds. Now, if you don't mind, I'd like to be with her in what might be her final days."

A few shutters clicked, but many more cameras were lowered in temporary shame.

Behind me, I heard a truck door slam. Crap. I had sort of forgotten about Scott. The last thing I wanted to do was get him involved in the middle of all of this. The mob turned and began snapping photos.

“Who’s the guy?” a voice asked as the group rushed him. Scott held up his hands to shield his eyes from the onslaught as he fought his way toward me.

“Are you and Morgan an item?”

Scott tried to find my eyes for a way he could be helpful, but he was just making things so much worse.

As they pressed in closer on him, I knew I had to save him from the spotlight.

“He’s here for my friend. He’s a nurse,” I said. “I’ll say it again. This is private property. I need you all to leave. I’m calling the authorities.”

“I’m already on the line with them,” Cassandra said, her phone pressed to her ear.

Reluctantly, they stopped their incessant cameras and grabbed their gear. When the last of them had driven away, Cassandra spun her attention on me.

“Now will you listen to me about installing a privacy gate?”

“I’m sorry,” I said, rubbing my hands over my face.

“What the hell is going on, Morgan?” she continued. “Is this the gay guy you’re lusting after?” She glared at Scott as my cheeks burned. “And who is this woman in your house?”

She huffed and put her hands on her hips. “I can’t help you fend off the press if you don’t tell me what you’re doing.”

I winced as I turned back to Scott who seemed just as confused as Cassandra. Normally, Bernard would be there to fix my epic blunders, but he was inside caring for the real Morgan. This was not my secret to tell, and yet, I didn’t see any way out.

“I’ll tell you both later. Right now, I need to get inside to see my friend. I’ll call you in the morning.” I said, trying to escape into the house.

“Like hell, you will. I am not leaving this house until you tell me who you have in there. I am your agent! I have to know what’s going on in your life, so I can protect you from exactly what happened today!” Her normally pale skin was starting to glow red with rage against the white dress she wore. Come to think of it, Cassandra was always in white. Maybe white was the new black?

“I’m waiting?” she hissed.

My mouth went dry trying to come up with a decent story. I didn’t enjoy lying to either one of them, but I didn’t know what else to do.

“I —” I began.

"It's okay," a deep voice said from behind me. "She wants Cassandra to come in."

I turned to see Bernard standing in the doorway. He looked as if he hadn't slept in days. The bodyguard's once perfectly manicured composure was now one of a broken man. His shirt was untucked. His tie hung loose, and his face revealed proof of exhaustion.

Cassandra raised her eyebrows at me, and back at Bernard before marching inside, leaving me alone with Scott.

"I won't ask," he said. "I can see this is not the best time for a conversation. You have a friend who needs you. Go. Be with her. I'll be around when you're ready to talk." He walked over to me and kissed me gently on the forehead. Before he went back to his truck, he gave one final squeeze of my hand.

I watched as he drove, wishing I were sitting next to him instead of, quite literally, standing in somebody else's shoes.

After his truck disappeared from view, I turned around and made my way back to a house I didn't live in, to play a part in a life that wasn't mine.

The house was cold as I pressed the door slowly closed behind me, though not in a temperature sense. In that way, it was quite toasty. The air felt different: somber somehow. All the natural lighting that had greeted me the day I ever walked into this house was now gone. In its place, the floor-to-ceiling windows were covered with navy blue bed sheets and other random rolls of fabric, leaving the room with an odd blue tinge to everything.

Bernard sat on the couch with Morgan's frail figure curled against his shoulder, her face obscured from view as though she was hiding from what was about to go down. I couldn't blame her.

"Okay, somebody needs to start telling me what's going on," Cassandra said, tapping the toe of her stiletto to the floor.

Bernard gently rubbed against the lump beside him. "It's like Jules said. Her friend is here, and she's dying of cancer." He barely got the words out.

Cassandra stood in the center of the living room glancing back and forth between Bernard and me. Clearly sensing I was the sanest of the two, she spun on her heal, tossing her hands into the air. "Who the hell is Jules?"

I turned a pitiful glance at Bernard, wondering if he had lost his mind by telling Cassandra my real name, but he simply looked at me with a vacant expression. He clearly didn't care about the ruse anymore. A weight lifted at being able to reveal the truth.

"*I'm* Jules," I said, brushing past Cassandra to sit next the ball of blankets.

"Oh, Jesus," she gasped, putting her hand on the bridge of her nose. "Is this some sort of identity crisis thing you're having now? Is that what you want to call yourself after the plastic surgery? *Jules?* Really?" Poor Cassandra sounded exasperated. "Are you seriously trying to reinvent yourself? Into this?" She gestured to me. "Honestly, Morgan, level with me. Tell me what's going on in that head of yours. Why are you acting like this and why the hell are you telling the media we have a dying person in the house?"

Just then, the blankets began to move.

"Lay off, Cassandra." Morgan's head popped out from the blanket. "Jules is just doing what I hired her to do."

Beside me, Cassandra gasped. Her eyes flung wildly between the two of us as though trying to make sense of what she was seeing.

"And she wasn't lying. I'm sick, Cassandra. Really, really, sick."

Chapter 21

It took several repetitions of the story before Cassandra would allow herself to believe any of it. I relayed it the third time when Bernard seemed to stop caring if she believed us or not. He simply wanted to be with Morgan, who I hated to admit, seemed even worse than just a few hours ago.

A small wastebasket beside her had to be emptied several times as we spoke. For someone who hadn't eaten all morning, it was inconceivable for her stomach to keep producing that much bile.

"So, I've been made a fool of, is that it?" Cassandra finally spoke. "Left out of the loop. You all thought it necessary to exclude me from this half-cocked idea, is that it?"

Morgan raised her head from the trash can, dragged her arm across her bottom lip. She forced a smile before flopping back onto the couch.

"Good old Cassandra, always able to find a way to turn the focus back on herself. Bravo." Morgan's words were weak, but the insult was dead on.

"Cassandra," I said, "why don't we leave them alone so she can rest? Maybe you and I can talk upstairs? Come up with a game plan?" I knew this fighting wasn't going to be good for Morgan and I wanted to do what I could to diffuse the situation.

It was clear from Cassandra's expression that she still felt the sting of Morgan's comment, but she didn't retort. Instead, she turned on her heel and stomped up the stairs, disappearing in a whirl of white into the screening room. I nodded to Bernard, who returned one in thanks, and I followed upstairs. It was time to tame the dragon.

I pictured finding her pacing the floors, ready to strangle me the moment I entered, but she was collapsed onto the couch with tears streaming down her face. Cassandra's reaction caught me off guard. In fact, if she hadn't seen me enter the room, I would have remained in the hall so she could compose herself. From the looks of it, however, maintaining her demeanor didn't appear to be an issue at the moment.

"So it's true? She's dying?"

"I'm not really sure," I hedged. "From what I was told, the medication she's on is her last option." I could still hear Morgan dry heaving even from upstairs. I walked over to the couch and sat down next to Cassandra. "All I know is that she didn't want to be stuck alone in some foreign hospital. She wanted to be with people who loved her. She wanted to be home." I paused and felt the weight of those words on my tongue. "I've never really had that. A place where I felt at home. Have you?" I'm not sure what prompted me to ask Cassandra such a ridiculous question, but it seemed like the sort of one she needed to be asked.

She didn't answer right away, but the faraway stare in her gaze told me she was pondering her answer. "I thought I did, once. I thought I *was* somebody's home. Turns out was more of a rental property." A single tear slid down her cheek before she brushed it off with a quick flick. Instantly, her composure returned. Her mask was firmly back in place. No further sharing of feelings would happen today.

"We have to plan," Cassandra said, standing up. "At least a dozen engagements are planned in the next few weeks. Television interviews, radio spots, the LA premiere. She has a movie to promote…and contractual obligations."

"Those obligations don't matter if she's dying."

Cassandra shook her head vehemently. "If this movie doesn't do well, she'll be dead anyway, at least to Hollywood." She let out a breath before coming close and sitting next to me. "She's not going to die." Her voice was confident. "That girl is a fighter. One of the strongest women in this business I've seen." She rubbed a hand on her chin, thinking. "This plan of hers, to use you as her doppelganger, it proves just how smart she is. It's worked so far. We'll just keep up the ruse, that's all," she said in a quick, frantic tone.

"No. You don't get it. I'm done. Game over. Morgan's sick. She doesn't need an agent right now. She needs to be surrounded by friends who love her."

Cassandra blinked a few times. "She hasn't got any friends. She doesn't have time for such foolishness."

I looked at her with a lost expression on my face. "That's incredibly sad. I don't know what I would do without friends in my life." But the moment I said it, I realized I was lying. I had lived these past few weeks in the same solitude Morgan had lived her whole life. Because of the contract, I had permitted Bernard to take away my cell phone, and with it, the connection to my friends and family. In my desire to make a few bucks, I had sacrificed the only part of my life that had been my rock, the thing I could always cling to when

I was drowning. I had allowed my friends and family to be pushed aside for a paycheck. It had all been so easy.

Macy and I used to talk *every* day…Rachel and Kim and I had brunch on Sundays, I went to the gym with Sandy at lunchtime…so many friends and I'd let it all slip away, without even meaning to.

While lost in thought, I found myself wondering if this was how it had begun for Morgan. When she started acting, had she sacrificed friendships thinking it would only be temporary. Had the lack of communication turned from weeks into years? Was that how she was left alone with only Bernard to hold onto? Was I doomed to go down that same road? Had the damage already been done?

"Well, if she doesn't have friends, we'll have to do," I said firmly.

"Do what?"

"Be her friends." She frowned at me. "Cassandra, this situation is more important than a stupid movie."

She opened her mouth as though ready to rattle on about the importance of said *stupid movie* but closed it.

"I don't know how to be someone's friend." Her statement was so simple and so brutally honest that my heart hurt for her.

“Follow my lead,” I said. “Although I’ve been a shitty friend of late, I’ve had a lot of practice.”

Her brief look of disbelief preceded a nod.

We went downstairs where I whispered our plan to Bernard. He looked up at me with a curious expression but nodded his consent. I grabbed Cassandra’s elbow and brought her outside with me.

“What are we doing?” she fussed, pulling her arm out of my grasp.

“We’re going shopping. Get in.”

I was in the car with the engine running before she even opened the door, no doubt debating whether she should go through with this or not.

As soon as she was buckled, I instructed her where to go. I really wanted to take the wheel of her Mercedes but had a feeling no one drove Cassandra’s car except her.

I had her pull into to the local mom and pop store that proudly boasted they rented DVDs. Their business must be the only place left on the planet that still did. I grew up with rental stores and mourned their loss with the advent of the digital world. If I could bring some of that nostalgia to Morgan, I was going to.

Cassandra sat in the car, gaping out the window with a horrified look on her face.

“What could we possibly need from there?”

“Movies!” I said, grinning like a fool and got out of her car.

A moment later, Cassandra was beside me, pulling hard on my elbow and practically hissing in my ear. It was clear she was not comfortable being inside the small shop.

“Would you please tell me why we’re buying DVDs when Morgan has access to any film she wants right at her fingertips?”

I rolled my eyes and browsed the New Release section with interest. “First off, we’re not buying them, we are only renting them, secondly, renting a DVD is different than searching an infinite digital library of choices. It’s better this way. Trust me.” The New Releases weren’t really what I was looking for, so I browsed the Cult Classics and instantly find the type of movies I wanted. I snatched up *Say Anything, Ferris Bueller’s Day Off, The Breakfast Club,* and *Dirty Dancing*. “We’re taking it old-school,” I said, wagging one of the DVDs mischievously in front of her face.

“Can’t wait,” she said with no apparent interest.

After we had paid for our rentals, we walked to the Shop and Go grocery store I had first visited when I got to town. I wondered absently if the mean girl who held my wine hostage would be working the register. Mercifully, some younger girl was at the counter.

I waved hello to a few of the open-mouthed locals on the sidewalk who still hadn't come to terms with a celebrity staying in their small town. I mean, she must have stayed at her mansion here before now. This couldn't have been the first time she'd stayed there. Then again, I doubt Morgan ever bothered to mingle with the locals during any stays.

"Good Lord. You cannot be serious," Cassandra said when we walked into the store. She jerked both hands to her chest as though afraid to touch anything.

I contained my snort "I guess you don't want to push the cart?"

Cassandra blanched. "Um, no."

Shaking my head at her, I grabbed one and headed down the first aisle, tossing in a few items as I went.

"What are we doing now?" Cassandra asked when I put in a stalk of celery.

"We're going to make her some homemade chicken noodle soup, and oh, yes! We can make cookies, too," I said while grabbing a roll of chocolate chip cookie dough.

"You want *me* to make her cookies?"

I grinned. "Yes. We're going to pamper her."

"Why? She has staff to make her food." Cassandra wore a sincere look of confusion on her face.

I stopped for a moment, grabbed her arm and gave it a gentle squeeze. "We're making it for her, Cassandra, because that's what friends do. They take care of each other."

She thought about it for a second and nodded.

"How about these mini-cucumber things?" she asked grabbing a jar of pickles.

"Pickles. Sure, why not?" Cassandra seemed relieved. I wondered, suddenly, if she'd ever had a pickle. If not, I was going to be in for a treat when she tried one. Bread and butter pickles were sort of an acquired taste.

When our cart was loaded with carbs, salty and sweet things and enough booze to kill a horse, we headed toward the single register at the front of the store.

That's when we encountered a husband and wife who were looking at me with wide eyes. Instantly, they began whispering to one another. You would think Morgan being here would be old news by now, but when you're in a town that doesn't even have a movie theater, I suppose a visiting movie star is a pretty big deal.

"Hi." I waved, which seemed to stop their whispering.

When the couple was out of earshot, I leaned over and whispered to Cassandra, "See, I'm still relevant. It's okay for a movie star to have a personal life." She just scoffed at what I deemed appropriate attention.

As we waited in line to check out, I looked around at the grocery store I'd once found repulsive. Today, it seemed rather quaint. It wasn't flashy or as spotless as it probably should be, but it got the job done. That was what Cassandra and I would do as well. While we might not be Morgan's oldest and dearest friends, it was up to us to show her as much joy as we could in what might be her last days. The gesture seemed important enough to invest the time, and I thought Cassandra was beginning to sense it, too.

I was placing the last items on the conveyer belt when Cassandra gasped.

"What?" I asked, though not really interested. She had made several such noises as she discovered items that horrified her, like the woman wearing socks with sandals in aisle three or the kid who was picking his nose next to the milk freezer.

"I think I know why you're still relevant. Especially here," Cassandra said.

Blowing the bangs out of my eyes with a quick burst from my lips, I checked the phone she held out to me, her mouth slightly ajar.

Staring back at us in full color on social media was a photo of Scott and I on the edge of his tailgate in a fully heated, R-rated kiss.

"Holy hell."

Chapter 22

I'm not sure how long I stood there scrolling through the pictures. They seemed to be trending on every social media platform I knew, and a few I hadn't. I wasn't sure if Scott subscribed to any of these, but it was bound to come across his path sooner or later. The paparazzi had captured every single one of our intimate moments. I'd never even seen them or heard a single camera click. Where the hell had they been?

That's when I realized what must have happened. This wasn't the work of the paparazzi but of one horny teenager with a cell phone. The angle of the picture puts the photographer right on the porch. He likely sent it to a few of his friends and then it went viral.

"So…something else you want to tell me about?" Cassandra asked pointing to the picture.

"Um…" I said, my voice weak and scratchy.

She crossed her arms over her chest.

"You told me that was one sided." One of her perfectly formed eyebrows shot up. "And that he was gay."

"Turns out he wasn't. Oops." I looked up at her with wide eyes. "What do I do?"

Cassandra pursed her lips. "Well, that all depends on the outcome you want."

"I want it to go away. I don't want Scott to be brought into the nightmare that has become my life. It's not fair. He didn't ask for this."

She threw her hands up in the air. "No one asks for stuff to happen to them, but like it or not, he's going to find out. You know what they say about honesty being the best policy." She frowned. "Unless, of course, it would hurt my client's image. Then, lying is always the way to go."

"I can't be honest with Scott. He still thinks I'm Morgan."

"Oh, right. Well, you're back to being screwed then."

"Remind me to never ask you for advice again."

Cassandra shrugged, a bored expression on her face, not once offering to help in any way with the groceries. "I'm sorry," she said. "I'm not sure what you want me to say. You can't hide this from him. He'll find out, of that much I know. The only question you need to ask yourself is, do you want him to find out from you, or on his own. Assuming, that is, he hasn't discovered it already. Who knows, maybe he'll be flattered by the attention. Some men are." Her eyes darkened. "Just ask Kade."

I shook my head a few times to clear my thoughts. Sure, I knew I'd have to talk to Scott, but right now, I was needed elsewhere. I had to keep my priorities straight.

"I'll call him tomorrow. We have soup to make."

Cassandra rolled her eyes. "Oh, goodie. Can't wait."

Morgan wasn't on the couch when we got back to the mansion, and my heart jumped into my throat, thinking the worst.

Bernard noticed my concerned expression and stood up to help with the bags.

"She's in the shower."

Relief washed over me. "Does that mean she's feeling better?"

Bernard rubbed his eyes. "No, she just threw up on herself."

"Oh." I looked at Cassandra who blanched. "Well then, she'll need her strength when she gets out of the shower. So do you. Why don't you go lie down? Cassandra and I will start the soup."

"*You're* making soup?" he asked Cassandra who just shot her hands up into the air, indicating she was no longer in control.

"This is all her idea. I'm just a victim," she said.

"It's really sweet of you, but I don't think Morgan will be able to keep any of it down," Bernard confessed.

"That's okay. Sometimes just the smell of a home cooked meal can help heal the soul." I grinned softly at him. "I don't mean to be rude, but you look like a zombie, Bernard. Go lie down for a few minutes. You won't be any help to her if you are exhausted."

He grumbled but eventually stalked off toward the bedroom, no doubt to wait for Morgan to get out of the shower. Poor thing hadn't stopped worrying since she'd gotten home.

Cassandra cleared her throat after he left. "Well, I don't know how to cook, so I'll just leave you to it." She took a step in the other direction, but I hooked her arm in mine before she could escape.

"It's high time you learned then."

For the next hour, I showed Cassandra how to cut a chicken breast, pausing every few moments to allow her gag reflex to wane. I had Cassandra bring a pot of water to a boil

(I had to explain how to do that too). Eventually, I started her chopping the veggies. I couldn't lie; it was fun to watch her prim and proper demeanor tear up when dicing the onions.

"Why in the hell would anybody willingly do this to themselves?" she said after the fifth attempt with the onion.

I knew she was in danger of chopping off her own fingers due to a number of tears clouding her vision, so I gave her the task of peeling carrots instead…after I showed her how to use a peeler.

"Seriously," I said, grabbing the peeler from her and showing her how to do it again. "How can you have lived your entire life without knowing the most basic of skills?"

"Easy. Servants and take-out."

I wanted to comment about how sad that was, but the way she said it made me feel that she knew the reality of it more than she'd admit.

We had just put the noodles in to cook when Morgan shuffled into the kitchen wearing a fluffy pink bathrobe with a matching towel wrapped atop her head.

"Wow, that smells amazing," she said. Her voice was rough from disuse, or just weakness. I couldn't tell which.

"Hey, you should be lying down. I'll bring you a bowl when it's ready," I said.

Morgan shook her head vehemently, causing the towel to loosen. She yanked it off and rubbed it absently against her wet hair.

"If I have to lie down again, I think I'll go mad. I practically had to threaten Bernard with the fireplace prod to get him to rest. The poor man is exhausted." She turned her head from side to side, checking around her kitchen as though seeing it for the first time. A soft smile touched her lips. "I was hoping maybe I could help."

I glanced over at Cassandra who was holding up a wooden spoon as if it were a dirty diaper. "You can stir the noodles," she said, clearly happy to be relieved of the duty. She hadn't considered, however, that Morgan might not actually have the physical strength for the task.

There was no way around it: Morgan looked like shit. Her skin appeared nearly see-through now. I was amazed she was able to stand at all, as weak as she must be, but I could also see the determination behind those eyes. She needed to feel useful. She needed a reason to fight.

"Fine," I said, nodding toward the spoon. "You can stay but only if you sit on this stool."

I brought one over from the island and plopped it down beside her. She sank into it willingly.

We worked in silence for a few moments, Morgan stirring, me chopping away happily, and Cassandra pretending to look busy as to avoid being assigned a new job. Finally, Morgan asked the question that was sure to be on all of our minds.

"If this doesn't end well. What is the plan?"

"We make a new batch of soup," I quipped, trying to avoid the conversation.

"That's not what I meant." Morgan sighed, putting her spoon down on the marble countertop.

I put my knife down as well. "I know."

"Well, I think you should keep up the disguise," Morgan said in a whisper. Cassandra cocked her head, her wheels already spinning.

"Um, no," I said, thwarting the attempt to hijack my life. "The jig is up. I'm not doing this anymore. You're back. I can go back to my normal, boring life."

"And if I die?"

I could see she was trying to be strong, but the tears were welling in her eyes.

"Then I will mourn for you, along with the rest of the world."

Morgan laughed. “The only one who will mourn for me is Cassandra, and that’s only because her paychecks will stop.”

Cassandra opened her mouth, affronted, but she wisely chose not to speak. This wasn’t the time for a discussion of loyalty.

“That’s not true, and you know it,” I said on Cassandra’s behalf.

Morgan stood up and walked over to the island, picked up the knife I’d been using and began to slowly chop a carrot but gave up when she didn’t have the strength to slice all the way through.

“Sure, my death will make headlines for a few days. People will show up to my funeral en masse, but not to pay their respects. Most will just make sure their photo gets taken. Funerals are a great way to get free publicity and show the world your human side. Isn’t that right, Cassandra?”

Cassandra bit her lip in confirmation.

“Don’t be fooled, Jules. Any weeping done the day I die will be crocodile tears.” Her voice barely croaked out, but the pain behind the words was as clear as day.

I had only been in her world for a short while, but it was long enough to recognize the truth. Hers was a hollow existence of false friends seeking to use her fame for their own gain.

"What about Bernard?" I countered, knowing I was betraying their unspoken relationship, but dammit, she needed a reason to hang on.

Morgan lifted her head up, her cheeks wet for a moment before she brushed rogue tears aside. "His will be the only real emotions that day."

Cassandra looked at Morgan. They traded an understanding of why they had kept their love secret.

I placed my hand against the blade as Morgan made a final attempt on the carrot.

"Then you need to fight your ass off…for him…if not for yourself."

That's when she lost it. Great blubbering tears sprang up from deep within her. It was as though all of the strength she had clung to in order to hold it together for Bernard had crumbled. What remained were the ugly, broken bits women didn't let other people see.

I did the only thing I could do. I wrapped my arms around her and let her weep. As Morgan sobbed, Cassandra stood a few feet away from us, clearly uncomfortable about what she was supposed to do. I motioned for her to join our huddle.

At first, she hesitated, clearly unsure where she was supposed to put her hands, but after a moment, I felt the strength of her arms closing in around her friend. Yes, Morgan was her client, but over the years, I think she had also become a friend. At that moment, I wondered if Morgan was Cassandra's only friend?

When the tears dried up, the misfit giggles began. It started with Cassandra complaining about her running mascara (which really was an atrocious sight) and eventually broke into fits of hysteria when a snot bubble formed on my left nostril. Not my proudest moment, but it sent us all into tears of laughter instead of sorrow.

At the sound of our maddening levels of cackling, Bernard rushed into the kitchen.

"What in the hell are you three doing?" he asked, clearly confused.

Morgan eyed me and smiled. "We're living, Bernard. Come, join us."

He stood there a moment, transfixed by her smile, and he obliged.

When the doorbell rang a few minutes later, breaking up our little cocoon of happiness, Morgan and Bernard quickly retreated into the bedroom to hide while Cassandra went to tell whoever it was to bug off.

I stayed in the kitchen to finish with the soup, humming softly as I dumped in the carrots.

"Um, I think it's for you," Cassandra said a moment later

I looked up at her and found a very angry looking Scott.

Shit.

Chapter 23

It was clear from the expression on his face, he had seen our kiss plastered everywhere. While a kiss like this would be benign in LA, here in Bucksville, NH, a public embrace between a movie star and one of their own would likely excite people.

I guess I could understand why he was angry. I didn't even want the attention, and I was being paid for it. Then again, it wasn't as if he didn't know who I was, or at least who I was pretending to be when he kissed me. Sure, the pictures were an invasion of privacy, but was it really so bad that people saw us kissing? I mean, was he trying to hide our relationship, or whatever the hell we were calling what we had? Unless…unless there was another woman in his life and that public kiss had blown his cover. My stomach began to churn.

"Mind telling me what's going on?" he asked, venom spewing out with each syllable.

"I don't know. Why don't you tell me?"

He crossed his arms over his chest.

"I think you know damn well what this is about."

Had to be another woman. It was the only reason he could be this pissed at me.

"It was just a kiss." I spat at him, matching his own anger. "So what if people took a picture of it? Sorry if I made someone else jealous."

He opened his mouth, flabbergasted. *BAM. Take that, jackass.*

"Are you serious?" His tone was accusatory which seemed very out of character for him, but then again, how well did I really know him?

"Look, if you're that upset about a kiss, that I rather enjoyed by the way, maybe you should just go." I forced my voice not to shake. Apparently to him, it was okay to kiss me as long as nobody found out. Man, he was just like Anthony. I was tired of being the dirty little secret.

Scott's face contorted from anger to shock then into disappointment. I could see there were a million things he wanted to say to me, but instead, he held his tongue. He didn't strike me as the sort of guy who got angry very often because it seemed as though he wasn't sure how to process his emotions.

"Maybe I *should* go. Clearly, you are not the person I thought you were." Though such a simple phrase, he had no idea how accurate he was.

"Yeah, well maybe you're not the person I thought you were, either." It was a childish retort, but it was the best I could come up with.

He put his hands on the white marble island, gripping the edges firmly as though trying to contain his composure.

"I'm sorry, how am I the bad guy in this situation?" he asked.

It was my turn to try and contain my anger. I threw my hands up in the air in exasperation. "You knew I was a public figure. I mean, something like this was bound to happen sooner or later. I'm sorry it happened without your knowledge, but this is the world you entered into when you met me. I thought you understood that." My lips trembled without my permission as I tried to talk past the tears. "It's not really fair to be upset with me about a kiss *you* initiated. It's not my fault the kiss we shared was leaked to the press." Scott looked at me, wounded. "I'm sorry if kissing me has embarrassed you or put you into the doghouse with some other girl. Trust me, you won't have to do it again." I tried not to make my voice crack, but it did anyway.

Tears had begun to cloud my vision, and I didn't want him to see that. I didn't want Scott to know he had gotten to me. I wasn't going to give him that satisfaction. With my shoulders thrown back, I plowed ahead to escape the kitchen and retreat to a place where I could fall apart out of his earshot. Before I could push past him, however, his arm reached out and grabbed my elbow, holding me firmly in place.

"I'm not angry about *our* kiss, Morgan."

I ripped my arm out of his hold, fuming.

"Well, what the hell *are* you talking about?"

He slumped his shoulder for a second, but then reached into his back pocket and pulled out a piece of newspaper. He tossed the scrap at me. Even though the picture was upside down, I knew instantly what it was. It was a picture of the premiere. Of Kade sticking his tongue halfway down my throat.

My eyes darted up just in time to see the hurt in Scott's eyes. "I asked you before I touched you…point-blank if you were spoken for. The next day, *the very next day*, you're kissing this guy for all the world to see," he said with a forced calm. "*That* is why I am upset, Morgan. You lied to me. You looked into my eyes and lied to me. You have a *boyfriend*. A famous one at that." He shook his finger at me. It was like a punch to the heart. "I knew you were hiding something, but I didn't think it was another guy." His face was so grief-stricken, it made me sick to my stomach. "I've had enough of women lying to me in my life already. I was a fool to think you'd be any different."

My mouth grew dry. He was right. I had completely spaced on Kade's kiss, that's how little it meant to me. I wanted to tell him that *Kade* had kissed *me*…that I hadn't asked for it, but it wasn't as though I tried to stop him either. I had allowed Kade to manhandle me. I had allowed the charade to continue. And for what? A job? I lowered my head in true shame.

"You're right. I lied to you," I said, the tears finally falling free. Maybe this was for the best. Maybe it was time I just cut my losses.

"My ex-wife slept around with half the town right under my nose, and no one told me." I looked up at him. It was the first time he had mentioned being married. A wave of jealousy surged through me. "Not one of my friends, no single person in town, bothered to clue me in. They knew, but they kept the lie going. They said 'It wasn't their place.'" His eyes bored into mine, the hatred there was palpable. "And to think, I almost fell for someone just like her." He rubbed his hands over his face before he spun around and left the kitchen.

His words gutted me. Suddenly, it didn't matter that I had a contract forbidding me from telling him the truth. I didn't care about the money. I only wanted him to know I wasn't the whore he believed I was, well, at least, not anymore.

I rushed after him, begging for him to stop until he opened the door and found a man standing there. His back was to us, but I could see he was a tall man in a familiar looking tan overcoat. I swallowed hard. That wasn't just any man.

"Anthony?" I gasped, unable to feel my legs.

Scott looked at Anthony as he turned around. "Who is Anthony?"

"I'm her boyfriend," Anthony said in an overt possessive tone that seemed to drip from his lips as he eyed Scott.

Scott gawked at me and laughed softly. "Of course, he is."

"Scott!" I shouted as he pushed out of the door.

I tried to rush after him, but Anthony grabbed my elbow and held me against his chest with both hands as I screamed for him to let go and for Scott to come back.

But he didn't. Scott got in his truck and took off, never looking back to see the tears streaming down my face.

"Goddamnit!" I cursed. Anthony let me go, and without thinking, I hauled off and punched him in the chest causing him to take a few steps backward. "What the hell are you doing here?"

"I brought him," another familiar voice said. I pivoted out into the driveway and saw Macy getting out of a car. She approached me with caution.

"Macy?" She gave me a small smile, and at that moment, I forgot all about Scott, all about Anthony, hell, I even forgot all about Morgan. My best friend was there, and somehow a hug from her was going to make all the difference. I raced down the steps and pulled her into an enormous embrace.

"Oh, my God. How did you find me? I've missed you so much! I can't believe you're really here." Each sentence stumbled over the last as we ran to hug each other.

Macy endured my barrage of questions and squeals of delight until Anthony had to ruin it all by clearing his throat.

"I hate to break up this happy reunion, but I think you have some explaining to do." Anthony twirled his thumbs around in his own judgmental way. With him standing up on the porch glaring down at me, I felt as though I was being scolded, and I hated it. Hated how this used to be the norm for me.

"*I* have some explaining to do?" I asked, flabbergasted. My leaving the state should have been the only explanation he required. "What are you doing here? How did you even find me? I didn't tell anybody where I went."

Macy shuffled her feet on the dirt, her dark curls bouncing as she moved. "The media sort of let us know. We went to New York first after we saw that picture of you and Kade. Holy hotness, by the way. The media was saying it was Morgan Malone, but you don't fool me. I knew it was you the second I saw you. I knew that postcard I got from you was bogus. England? You? Fly across the ocean? Please. Only, I couldn't figure out *why* you were parading around pretending to be some movie star. When I told you to milk the fact that you looked like Morgan Malone, this totally wasn't what I meant. Jules, you could get in serious trouble pretending to be her." I bit my lip. "Seriously. She's gonna sue your ass when she finds out. That's why I came. I had to find you and smack some sense into you before you got arrested." She glared at me before gesturing to Anthony.

"I even went and asked this dumbass if he knew what you were up to, which was a mistake, 'cause the asshole insisted he come with me to track you down." I snarled at her blatant disloyalty. "What? The man has access to a private jet. I don't. I just wanted to find you, Jules. You stopped calling…you ignored my messages…you started pretending to be a movie star…I was worried," she said as though it was the only explanation she needed to give me. And really, it was. I would have tracked her ass down too if the situation had been reversed.

"When we saw the photo of you in New Hampshire with that lumberjack hottie—you'd better tell me the dish on that later—we took off like a bandit to find you. It wasn't hard. The picture told us the town you were in and locals were more than happy to rat out where you lived." Macy looked up at the mansion, clearly impressed with the new digs.

"I bet they were," I said. "Okay, fine, that explains how you found me, but why are *you* here?" That question I directed at Anthony. Macy tracking me down made perfect sense, but him joining the hunt did not.

Anthony sauntered down the steps and walked over to me. He reached out a hand and cradled the side of my face with it. It was odd, the smoothness of his manicured hands felt wrong compared to Scott's slightly callused ones. Anthony's hands seemed dirty despite their pristine condition.

"We're here because we were worried about you. You took off without any explanation."

I threw my head back to get my face out of his hands. "That's not true. Macy knows why I left…to get away from you. To start my life over."

Anthony took my hands. "That's what I'm here to offer you, babe. A do-over." He tucked a strand of my hair behind my ear. "I'm leaving her."

"Yeah, right."

"No, it's true. I sent her the papers before I came out here. I realized that without you near me, I didn't feel complete. I missed you and knew I needed to do whatever I could to get you back, so I finally left her. I packed my bags and have a rental all lined up for us when we get back." I took a step back from him, completely shocked. This was what I'd waited three years for him to say. He had done it. He had left his wife. This was all I'd ever wanted. Somehow, I had imagined it would feel different.

“Come home with me, babe. We’ll start over.”

“What about your wife, your kids…your unborn child?”

He made a dismissive expression. “The kid will be well provided for, as will the rest of them. Come back to me. We can live the life we always dreamed of.”

Everything in my head turned fuzzy. I couldn’t believe he was saying those words, now, after all this time of me wishing we could be together. Here he was, *fighting* for me. That’s all I had ever wanted from Anthony—for me to matter to him. And now I did.

What about Scott?

What about him? He hates me. Even if I did manage to make amends with him, I’d let him down eventually. It’s what I did. Anthony was the only one who didn’t poke fun at me for being a temp. He didn’t care that I moved twice a year. He didn’t care that I meandered. Maybe this was the real reason I came out here, to see if he would follow me? And he did. That had to mean something, right?

“Julie,” I blinked a few times as I heard my name being called from behind.

“I need a word with you,” Bernard said.

“Who is this dude?” Macy asked, clearly confused.

I took a step closer to Anthony, ready to sink back into his arms. He wanted me. Finally, somebody wanted me.

"Now, Ms. Green. I have to insist. It's urgent."

That snapped me out of it. Something must be wrong with Morgan. I looked up at Bernard and nodded once.

"I'll be right back. Stay here. There's still a lot I need to say," I said. Anthony bowed and reached out to kiss my hand. The gesture used to give me butterflies, but now it fell flat.

It must be because my head hadn't wrapped around the fact that any of this was real. That would change with time. I'd see this as the gift that it was soon enough.

I hurried up the stairs to see what the situation was with Morgan. Bernard held the door open for me, glaring the whole time at Anthony as he did.

Once I was inside, he closed it, leaving me alone with Morgan as he stood guard outside. She was sitting by the window, the sheet had been pulled aside just a bit so she could look out.

"I've been watching the show," she said. "Who's the guy?"

I smiled, relieved she wasn't dead.

"That's Anthony. The guy I left when I came out here. We were together three years. Well, kind of."

"He looks older than you."

I bit my lip. "Yeah. He is. A bit. He's fifty-five, but that's only like a thirteen-year difference. He's really smart, active, you know? Fit. He's the CEO of a pharmaceutical company—"

She nodded as she looked out the window again. "I noticed he's wearing a wedding ring." Her voice was eerily calm. Not judging me, just stating the cold, hard facts.

My shoulders slumped. Morgan patted the cushion beside her on the window seat.

"He is. Well, he won't be for long. He's getting a divorce." I ventured another smile.

She nodded again. "Did I hear you say his wife is pregnant?"

"Yeah," my face reddened. "With their third, but he said he was going to provide for it so…" I trailed off.

Morgan's head cocked to the side. "*It?* This is a child you're talking about. One that is going to need a father, not just a paycheck."

Guilt flooded into me.

"Jules, do you hear yourself? Do you actually hear the words coming out of your mouth? He's fifty-five. He's married. He has a family, another child on the way. Are you seriously going to leave here with him?"

My eyes began to tear up hearing the truth of it all out loud.

"He wants me. He came out here to bring me back."

Morgan reached over and took my hand.

"What are you running from, Julie? What is so terrifying here that you are willing to go back to the life you just escaped?"

Blinking back tears, I checked over my shoulder, somehow expecting someone to be there, listening in on this very private conversation.

"It's too stupid." I sniffled.

"Somehow, I doubt that. Tell me. What has got you so spooked?"

I let out a long breath. "I'm scared that…that I'll never find an anchor." The words spilled out before I could consider the truth they would reveal. "I've never felt that I belonged anywhere. My dad was in the navy when I was young, so we moved a lot. That carried over into my adult life I guess. I've moved every six months or so. I get antsy. I can't seem to stay put. My relationship with Anthony was the longest I've ever had with a guy. Now that has to mean something, right?"

"I'm not sure I'd use the term relationship for the affair you had."

"But we've been together so long…"

"That doesn't make him your anchor. Just your safety net," she said gently. "For someone to be your anchor, they have to be immovable even when *you* are the storm." She reached over and patted my knee. "Somehow, I don't think Anthony fits that description."

"So, what? I'm supposed to let him go and just continue to stay adrift forever?" I hiccupped.

Morgan smiled. "No. I think your *real* anchor left a moment ago in a jealous rage."

I scoffed through my tears. "Scott hates me."

"Only because he doesn't know the truth. Once he does, you'll get past this."

"Yeah, but I can't tell him the truth, can I? At least Anthony would take care of me. He'd make sure I was provided for!"

Morgan gave me a sad smile. "Like he's going to provide for his wife and kids?"

At that, I began to cry. “I don’t know what I’m supposed to do, Morgan. I’ve waited for so long to Anthony to want me and now that he does…”

“You want someone else,” she finished for me.

I wiped the tears from my face. “It doesn’t matter what I want. Scott will never forgive me.”

“He’s jealous, Jules. Jealousy can make men say and do some pretty horrific things. Let him cool down, but then tell him the truth. All of it.”

“But…I can’t.”

“All of it.” She stood up, leaning against the window for support as she did. “Consider the confidentially contract null and void for him.”

I stared up at her, in shock about what she was saying.

“Humor me, Jules. I might be dying here.”

I laughed despite the tears.

“And tell that ass-wipe to get off my property.”

I let out another laugh and hugged her.

She pulled me back and took me by the shoulders.

“When he leaves, clean yourself up and go find Scott.”

I let out a shaky breath.

“You can do this, Jules. You owe him the truth.”

I nodded once. Yes. Yes, I did.

Chapter 24

Morgan left me alone with my thoughts, so I took a moment to compose myself and re-grow my backbone. Thanks to my chat with Morgan the situation was perfectly clear and utterly humiliating. I had almost fallen for Anthony's lines again. He had come so close to pulling me back into the game. I was ashamed of myself.

But no more. No more letting him worm his way into my heart. I stood up tall and felt stronger already.

With renewed purpose, I marched to the door and opened it. Bernard stood at the ready, seeming to wait for a signal from me to physically remove the trash. "It's okay, Bernard. I've got this."

He stepped aside, arching his eyebrow at me. Brushing past him, I headed down the steps and stood about a foot away from Anthony. Macy had both hands on her hips, no doubt ready to smack me if I got in the car with him.

"You have any bags you need to pack?" he asked, trying to reach in to give me a hug. I held out my hand.

"When I asked you to stay earlier it was because I had words to say, I never said they would be kind ones."

Out of the corner of my eye, I saw Macy's face light up.

"Baby, what do you mean? I gave you what you wanted. I left her."

I looked up at him and laughed.

"After three years. All that time, I waited to be important to you. To matter to you, to come first, and it took me traveling across the country for you to decide you missed me."

Anthony's face hardened at the accusation. "Jules, you have never been my second choice. You know how badly I wanted to divorce Claire. It was just…complicated."

Macy hummed an "Mmmhmmm," for me.

I locked eyes with Anthony. "Actually, it's not complicated at all. You were a phase in my life, a stepping stone. I can see that now, You allowed me to see what it is I want in a relationship, and it's no longer you. I've moved on. And so should you. I'd like you to leave now." With those words, the veil of shame that had been draped over my shoulders during our entire relationship vanished. It wasn't just words. I really meant it—didn't want him anymore. Even if Scott and I never made amends, it didn't matter. I knew what I wanted in a relationship, and what I didn't. A strong sense of freedom came with that knowledge.

Anthony's face grew hot with anger. He saw the shift in my attitude, too.

"You are making the biggest mistake of your life."

I shook my head. "No. The biggest mistake of my life was not leaving you sooner. Now I'll say it again. Please leave."

I crossed my arms over my chest. His words had no affect on me any longer. His control over me had vanished, and he knew it.

"Fine. Let's go, Macy." He reached out and put his slimy arm around her shoulders, almost as though he were staking a claim on his newest conquest.

"Oh, hell no," Macy said, stepping out from under his arm. "I'm not going anywhere with you. I'm saying right here with my girl."

Anthony glared at Macy.

"I asked *you* to leave, not her." I stepped in front of my best friend, shielding her from his attempted claim on her.

"Fine then. Have it your way. But you'll come crawling back. You always do." With that, he got in his car and drove out of my life.

Jackass.

"Girl, that took some serious balls!" She came over and gave me a massive hug. It felt so wonderful to have her back with me. Until she pulled away and nodded toward the mansion. "You have got some stories to tell me. Starting with why the hell you never called me back."

"You're right. I don't have my phone anymore. I—I sort of needed to be out of Anthony's reach, and me out of his," I said, realizing how true the statement was. "I'm sorry that meant becoming MIA to you as well."

She reached out and took my hand as my eyes lingered toward the driveway. "He can't hurt me anymore." My voice was strong. Determined. I liked it.

Macy smiled. "I can see that. You really are over him, aren't you?"

I focused on Macy's hopeful eyes. It was corny, but I was proud to answer her.

"I am. I honestly and truly am."

Her grin was infectious. "About damn time."

I knew I had bridges to repair, truths to tell, but for now, I wanted to hug my friend and try to repair some of the damage I had caused when I shut her out.

"Sorry to interrupt this little reunion, but we have a conference call that simply cannot wait any longer," Cassandra said from the porch in her full managerial tone.

Macy turned to look at me, her eyebrows disappearing into the coarse curls that revolved around her head.

"Who is that?" Macy asked.

How was I going to explain this? "Macy, this is Cassandra, she's an agent…Cassandra, I'd like you to meet my best friend from LA, Macy Watts."

Cassandra looked down at me with an expression of warning.

"She deserves to know what's going on, " I said, biting my lip. My world was crashing into Morgan's, and I didn't see any other options.

Cassandra's mouth twitched before she clucked her teeth together in resignation.

"Why don't we just invite the paparazzi in while we're at it?" She huffed, throwing her hands up in the air, but went back inside with no further argument to stop our entrance.

I turned back to Macy and looped my arm through hers. “Come on, I want you to meet someone.”

Macy gave me an odd look but followed along beside me. The moment we came inside, Bernard stood up, trying to shield Morgan as she lay on the couch.

“What’s going on?” he asked, his arms spread out wide in a feeble attempt to hide her.

“It’s over, Bernard. I’m done. I don’t want to keep doing this. It’s not right.” His nostrils flared, but I continued into the room. “I had to lie to the only people in my life who are actually important to me, and for what? To live in a cushy house for a few months?”

“You signed a contract,” Bernard reminded me.

I nodded. “I did, but…it’s not worth it. I don’t want to play this game anymore.”

Morgan peeked out from behind Bernard. Her eyes seemed a little brighter than they had been in the morning. I think she was proud of me.

“Um,” Macy tapped my shoulder, “Who’s that?”

“I’m Morgan Malone. Who are you?”

Macy let out a small laugh and then promptly passed out.

Chapter 25

I would like to have said her blackout was quaint and eloquent, but alas, Macy fell at a weird angle and managed to land on a glass end table, sending shards in every direction. By the time she hit the floor, my best friend was covered in superficial cuts that I tended to easily enough with a handful of Band-Aids.

"Ow," Macy said after she came to.

"I don't think I've ever seen you faint before." I gasped, pulling open another Band-Aid.

"Here, clean this up," Bernard said, coming into the room with a broom and handing it to Cassandra.

"Me?" She balked.

Bernard's voice was firm. "Yes, you. You don't want your sick client to step on glass do you?"

Silently fuming, Cassandra took the broom and attempted to sweep up the glass.

If I hadn't been so worried about my friend, I would have laughed my ass off. Cassandra had clearly never used a broom before either. She was like a toddler, making a bigger mess than the one she was trying to clean up. Eventually, Bernard shoved her aside and took over, so the glass didn't end up scattered all over the floor.

"So what, exactly, is the deal, then? Are we just telling everyone who walks up to the door who you are now?" Cassandra asked, brushing away hair that had fallen into her face, something that rarely happened in her perfectly put-together life. I could tell she was extremely uncomfortable with the uncertain path that lay ahead of us. I wasn't all that collected about the situation myself.

"Calm down, Cassandra," Bernard scolded.

Morgan sat up a little higher. "I'm sorry I scared you, Macy. I know I must look a fright."

Macy's eyes grew wide. "No. No, that's not it at all. I just—"

Morgan smiled. "It's just you weren't expecting to meet a movie star today?"

"Um, yeah," Macy admitted. "I didn't know the two of you actually *knew* each other. I mean, I figured out that she was pretending to be you, but I didn't know you two were like pals." There was no mistaking the glare she sent my way for not revealing such an epic truth to a friend.

"I *didn't* know her," I said. "Not until I got here." I checked on Cassandra who just threw her arms up into the air in surrender. "Someone mistook me for Morgan in the grocery store and it all sort of snowballed from there." I plopped onto the couch beside her, relieved to finally be able to tell her the truth.

Bernard continued the story from that point, clearly understanding I wasn't sure if it was my place to reveal the full truth. The small squeeze on his hand from Morgan permitted Bernard to tell her everything—even about the cancer.

"Wait, so you're dying?" Macy asked Morgan. I winced at the crassness of her remark. Morgan seemed non-pulsed and even gave Macy a small chuckle.

"Well, that remains to be seen. The doctor told me I would only have a few months to live if this treatment didn't work."

At that, everyone was silent, save for a small sniffle from Bernard. Morgan pulled back the covers, and stood up, brushing off Bernard's attempts to help her. There was a determination to her whittled frame. We all watched as she crossed the living room, pulled out a drawer from the table against the windows, and removed a pad of paper.

"I guess it's time I made a will."

Bernard stood up and went to her. "You don't need to do that now."

"Don't I? I need to get my affairs in order." Morgan pressed the bridge of her nose with her fingers. "These last days would have been a great end to a memoir." She laughed. "If only I were a writer."

At that, Macy perked up. And I knew exactly why.

"No, Macy," I began.

"But it would be epic. Profound. Readers would snatch it up."

Morgan glanced over at us. "What would be?"

I let out a long breath. "Macy works in publishing."

Macy nodded emphatically. "We could do it. The two of us. I could ask you questions, take down notes. I'm actually a ghostwriter. You'd be surprised, hardly any of the memoirs of famous people were actually written by them. It could be the legacy you leave behind. Your parting words to the world—" Macy was in full planning mode, not even noticing that what she was saying was insensitive.

“Or, it could be your ticket to renewed stardom for when you recover,” chirped Cassandra, grinning with a calculated smile.

Morgan looked at Macy, then back at Cassandra, as though she was seriously contemplating it.

“I’ll do it on one condition,” Morgan said. “I tell the truth. All of it. Even about Jules.”

Morgan turned to me for approval.

“This isn’t my story, Morgan. It’s yours. It’s up to you if you want to tell it. Whatever you think is best.” I wasn’t going to deny a potentially dying woman’s last request.

Morgan nodded. “Fine. I’ll do it.” She smiled and stood a little taller. I wondered if this might be good for her. This book might be something to give her purpose, something to look forward to.

Macy wasted no time. She dug into her purse, pulled out her recorder and trusty notepad and began a gentle onslaught of questions. It was fun to see Macy in her element. Her entire demeanor changed. She was all business now as she worked in her journal, asking questions in a very Barbara Walters manner. That is, until Macy started sneezing her head off.

"I'm sorry." She wheezed. "I don't usually do this." Another one, and another right behind that. Now, a normal person sneezing would be no big deal, but Macy was far from dainty when she did. "This is so embarrassing," she said, digging into her purse for a tissue to clean up the spray all over her chest.

That's when Tripod decided to make an entrance, jumping onto Macy's lap, purring the whole time. Macy's sneezing became even more frantic.

"Macy, are you allergic to cats?" I asked. The fact that I didn't know this about my best friend was rather disturbing, but then again, neither one of us had ever owned a cat.

She sneezed again. "Um, maybe?"

I hurried across the room and scooped Tripod into my arms. She wiggled out of my grasp and dug her tiny claws into my shoulders, climbing up around my neck for a better view. "It's okay. I need to take her home anyway."

It was time to have that talk with Scott. Morgan and I exchanged a knowing nod of support as Bernard stood up, dug inside his pocket and handed me his keys. "Be careful with the leather." I suppressed a smile. Clearly, he hadn't seen the damage Tripod had done to his back seat already.

I snatched the cashmere throw from its perch on the wingback chair and brought it and the kitten into the car. I laid out a nice little blanket for Tripod with the throw, but naturally, the second I started the ignition, she was off the seat and wandering around in the back, tiny claws puncturing the leather again. *Oops.*

Once I was on the road, it dawned on me, I didn't know where to go. I had no idea where Scott lived. I supposed I could just start asking around town, the same way Macy had found me. But I didn't want the locals to gossip anymore about us than they already had.

While debating my next move, I noticed the limo had a small black screen. I touched it, and it sprung to life, opening up a web browser as a hello. The limo had a hot spot. Of course, it did. I pulled over and did a quick search for Scott Jacobs in Bucksville, New Hampshire. I assumed the search would prove fruitless, or at the very least only show the hospital where he worked, but to my great surprise, his full address and phone number were displayed right there on the screen.

"Well, hot damn."

I pulled out and began the four minute drive to his house. There was little point in trying to plan out what I was going to say because I really had no clue what I was going to tell him.

"Your destination is on the left," the GPS announced way sooner than I was ready for. Letting out a nervous breath, I pulled over to the side of the road and parked on the street in front of his house, unsure of what I was supposed to do next.

Scott's truck was in the driveway, and there was a single light on inside the quaint cape-style home even though the sun was still fairly high in the sky. He was home. No way to dodge this bullet now.

As I gathered my courage, I took a look at his house. It was cute. The sort of place people might dream about living in one day when they were old and grey. And yet, there was something off about it. While the house itself seemed well-maintained, no chipping paint, no broken shutters or anything, the place had a definite un-manicured feel that lingered. I cocked my head to the side, trying to pinpoint what it was.

His house looked sad, somehow. Maybe it was because there were no curtains hanging in the windows or that the window boxes contained only dead flowers, all shriveled up and decayed from their former glory. It was odd because the shrubs were neatly trimmed and yard looked recently raked. There was no chipping paint on the house. It was a juxtaposition of household maintenance. Why keep only some things pristine if the finishing touches were left to rot?

Finishing touches…the things a wife might have tended to. That had to be it. Scott had maintained his tasks, but not the items his ex-wife had most likely cared for. Whether that was because it hurt too much to be reminded of her or if it was neglected out of pure spite, I had no way of knowing, but noticing it made my heart ache.

I didn't like that he had been hurt before, but what I hated more was the thought that I had made it worse.

"Confession time," I whispered to the rearview mirror.

Grabbing the blanket from the floor, I scooped up Tripod into the folds of the throw and carried the fur ball to the front door. With shaking legs, I knocked on the red door.

I heard a few footsteps, followed by a hushed curse word, confirming he had seen me through the window. It was too late to run now.

A moment later, the door flung open. The hurt on Scott's beautiful face was almost too much to take.

"How did you find me?" he asked without meeting my eyes. He focused his attention safely on my knees.

"GPS." I shrugged. I held up the squirming blanket. "Tripod missed you."

He scoffed.

"*I* missed you," I said.

At that, he looked up.

I cleared my throat. "I want to try and explain. You're right, I lied. But there is so much more to this story you need to know."

He stood up taller and crossed his arms over his chest. "Why, so I can forgive you?"

"No." I shook my head vehemently. "So you'll know just how right you are to hate me."

Tripod began to escape her cocoon.

"Well, you better come in before she runs off and gets hit by another car," he said, pushing his door open wider to let us both in. I thought back on that fateful day when this little shit had brought us together. It seemed like a lifetime ago.

"Just give me five minutes, and I'll go," I said. "After that, you'll never have to see me again." I realized in the moment that I meant it. I would confess the truth and leave. I knew what it was like to be lied to and understood, first hand, how lies broke bonds. I had built the foundation of our relationship with them, and for that, there could be no forgiveness. “Please,” I begged. I had to get this off my chest.

“Fine. Five minutes.”

He opened the door wider and let me in as my heart lodged in my throat. Tripod leapt out of my arms and bounded down Scott’s hardwood hallway as fast as her little pink cast would allow her. She tripped a few times but bounced back quickly, disappearing into another room, leaving the two of us alone.

“So,” he said, gesturing toward the living room, “before you say anything, I want you to know that I am working really hard to show compassion and understanding right now. Admittedly, when my wife left, I was not as reverent as I would have hoped, so I am trying to learn from that mistake by allowing this conversation to take place.”

He closed his eyes for a moment before he led us into the living room which was highlighted in rich, dark wood. A large bay window on the right let the late afternoon sun fill the room. The house was tidy and not at all like the bachelor pads I’d seen with other guys I’d dated. It was the home of a man who took pride in his surroundings. That wasn’t to say it seemed like a museum…it felt lived in. Homey. I slunk into the proffered mahogany-colored sofa and placed my hands on my lap. Scott sat in a recliner far away from me.

"I'm trying not to let my anger get in the way of actually hearing what you have to say, but you need to know that I am. Very angry. But to be honest, I'm madder with myself than I am with you."

"Why should you be mad? This is so my fault, not yours," I said.

"I should have been more upfront with you about how important honesty was to me. It probably seems like such a trivial thing to be mad about, but I know how fast the lies can pile up, and I just don't want to do that to myself again." His voice was measured as though letting the words come out slowly, so they didn't bubble over as rage. "I can't go down that road again."

"I need you to know that I don't blame you *at all* for being upset with me. I'm pretty angry at myself, too."

That admittance seemed to calm him down. He shifted back further in his chair. "Okay, how about you tell me why I have a right to be so upset?"

I swallowed. My throat was dry. "I don't know where to start."

"How about at the beginning, Morgan?"

I nodded. The beginning. “Well, for starters, my name’s not Morgan.”

He didn’t seemed fazed by this knowledge. “I didn’t figure it was.”

I gawked up at him, shocked. *Had he known? He suspected this bait and switch from the beginning?*

“I mean,” he continued. “Not many stars have the name they are born with, do they? They need to sound more Hollywood, right?”

“Ah, no,” I said, shifting to face him. “I mean that in the literal sense. I’m not an actress. I’m not famous. I’m not Morgan Malone at all.” That got his attention. He appeared puzzled for a long moment.

“I think we might need a drink for the rest of this conversation.” He got up, walked over to a glass-enclosed bookcase and pulled out a bottle of Jack Daniels. He came back with two glasses, poured a few fingers full and handed one to me. I downed it in one gulp.

“Liquid courage,” I said, apologetically.

Scott nodded as he took a small sip from his glass. “Okay, tell me then. Who the hell are you?”

In all honesty, I had no flipping idea.

Chapter 26

The whiskey was still warm in my throat as I rubbed my palms on my pants.

"Right. Well, I guess I'll start with the basics." I said to the well-loved hardwood floors. "The first time we met, the night you almost killed the kitten? That was the real me. Julie Green."

"Jules," he said, remembering.

"Right." I swallowed down the lump in my throat and plowed on with my story. "Okay, so I guess I'll start with before we met…Um…let's see…I lived in LA most of my adult life working as a temp." I closed my eyes for a moment before checking to see his reaction. He had leaned forward, as though waiting for a punch line.

"You're a temp…" he finally said, nodding for me to continue.

"Yes. But it wasn't just my job that was temporary. It was my whole damn life." I glanced over at him for a moment before I went on. "I never stayed in the same apartment for long, six months tops. After that, I *had* to find a new place—something better, you know? Something, anything, to get me out of my current rut. It was the same with my jobs. Whatever boring and monotonous task I was assigned didn't matter because my work didn't define me. I was only there for a few months or weeks. *It wasn't my life*. It was just temporary." I got up and criss-crossed the room to a chair from where Scott was and sat. His hands were pressed together resting on his chin.

"While I was out there, I fell hard for a man in LA, the guy you met, Anthony."

"Your boyfriend." I glanced up and saw Scott's face pinch in anger for a moment.

"No. He was never my boyfriend. Not really. Having a boyfriend implies that someone cares about you in a meaningful way." I sighed before admitting the horrible truth. "He's married." I shook my head. "He was going to leave his wife for me. How special was I?" I let out a sad laugh. "For three years, he was going to leave his wife. And I believed him." I rubbed my hands over my face, mostly to try to wipe off the shame I felt lingering there. "And then one day, I woke up. I realized what a fool I'd been. I knew I had been brainwashed into thinking he cared about me, but in reality, all he was concerned about was keeping his mistress."

I stood and walked over to the dining room. At the end of the room was a large hutch filled with decorative plates and wedding china. It was so peaceful here.

"It's stuff like this," I said, gesturing to the china cabinet. "I never had shit like this…massive pieces of furniture or mortgages or family…the kind of things that keep a person anchored to one place. No. I always needed to be mobile." I held back tears that were forming. "Absolutely nothing tied me to LA. Sure, I had friends, but they all had real lives, you know? They had careers. They had condos, families. They had invested in stocks. They had legitimate significant others. But me? I was the only one who was lost."

I walked back over to the coffee table and poured myself another glass. After a hearty sip, I sat back down on the couch.

"So you left LA?" Scott asked, clearly trying to get to where I became Morgan Malone.

I nodded.

"Why here?"

I shrugged. "Why not here? I didn't care where I went. I just wanted to get as far away from that life as possible. New

Hampshire just happened to be as far as my credit card would take me."

Scott shifted in his chair, and his expression had softened, but he was still guarding his emotions. For good reason. The best was yet to come.

"The house I rented…the house where you first met me? I had no idea how I was going to pay the next month's rent, but it didn't matter at the time. I had escaped Anthony's hold on me. I was going to start a whole new life." I frowned. "I had no job lined up, no skills that could be used in small town America and no friends to help out. I had no idea what I was doing."

"So, you came out here to start a new life," he said. "I can understand that, but why take on the life of a movie star? Why steal someone's identity?"

"Because she asked me to."

Scott cocked his head to the side.

"It sounds ridiculous, but it's true. Morgan Malone paid me to be her."

"And just why would she do that?" He didn't believe me. Hell, I wouldn't have either.

"I don't know how closely you follow the entertainment world," I began.

"Not at all," he clarified, confirming my suspicion.

"Well, you know those tabloids I told you about that day in my rental house? The ones that raked me over the coals about the plastic surgery I had, well, Morgan had?" I was confusing myself in what was truth and what was lie.

"I remember, yes."

I nodded. I did too, vividly. That was the day he had said I was beautiful.

"What I didn't tell you is that the surgery wasn't corrective at all. It was for serious medical reasons." I hedged about how much to tell him but remembered Morgan had told me to tell it all. "She has skin cancer." I looked up at him as he tried to absorb the information. "She was going to need several months to recover from the medications they gave her. The timing was awful. She was about to premiere a movie and was on every magazine cover. She couldn't back out of the limelight or her career would be ruined." I paused to catch my breath. "So when she found out that her virtual doppelganger had shown up in the same town as one of her vacation homes, she hired me to take over her life."

Scott made a noise of disbelief.

"I know it sounds crazy. Believe me, I thought I was on some sort of secret camera show when Bernard approached me. But that day the limo picked me up? That's when I found out about Morgan. She had literally tracked me down." I shook my head remembering it all. It had happened so fast. "The plan was only for a few months…just until she healed. It was supposed to be me and my thoughts hanging out in her mansion, making sure the press got a few shots here and there, but it sort of all went haywire. I had to go to that movie premiere and pretend I was famous! It was hell! Absolute hell! The kiss you saw with Kade—" Scott's nostrils flared a bit. "Yes, that was me, but *he's* the one who stuck his tongue down my throat. As much as I wanted to punch his lights out, I couldn't because I was *Morgan Malone*. He was her boyfriend, at least in the media's eyes. I was just playing my part, the part she paid me handsomely for," I said, deflated.

I watched as Scott tried to absorb the details. I knew it was a lot to take in. Biting my lower lip, I wondered how best to continue.

"You have to understand, this was just another temp job for me…a solution to my lack of cash problem. It was going to be what I needed to fund my new life," I said, throwing my hands in the air. "None of this other stuff was supposed to happen! I wasn't supposed to meet you or help rescue a damn kitten, and I sure as hell didn't intend on falling in lo—" I stopped short. My eyes bulged. *What had I almost said?*

"I see." Scott didn't say anything else. He just sat there, staring at me. His silence said it all. He didn't feel the same. Or, if he had at one point, he didn't any longer.

Right. Of course. I had screwed it up.

"Well. That's it. That's what happened, so I'm just gonna go now. I promise you won't have to see me again." I set the empty glass on the coffee table with a clinking sound that echoed off the walls. With tears blurring my eyes, I grabbed my purse and bolted for the door. This was just one more failure to add to the long list I'd gained over the years.

I was going to need to put some serious distance between us. Even farther than I had with Anthony. Maybe it was time to get over my fear of flying across oceans. No place seemed far enough, though. I had a feeling this pain was going to follow me like a shadow.

"Morgan," I heard Scott say as I left the living room. "I mean Julie, dammit, wait up."

He was about to try and let me down easy. There was no way I could stick around for that. I didn't need his pity. I didn't need anything from him. I just needed to leave.

I swung the kitchen door open and hurried out onto the porch. In my rush, I opted to bypass the three steps down to the sidewalk, clearly forgetting I was no longer a coordinated twelve-year-old.

As soon as I took the leap, I knew I would be landing on my ass. Trying to alter the rules of gravity, my arms pinwheeled in an effort to balance myself, which only managed to change the direction I fell, so instead of landing on the dense cushion of the lawn and my backside, I landed flat on my right ankle on the concrete walkway instead. The resounding snap confirmed my idiocy.

I screamed out in pain as I reached for the injured foot, which was already beginning to swell.

"God!" I groaned, closing in on myself in agony. After the first wave of nausea had passed, I opened my eyes and saw Scott running toward me. "I'm all right," I hissed, trying to stand up. The pain was blinding.

"Don't move," Scott said, kneeling beside me.

"I said I was fi—i—ne." I gritted my teeth together and tried to crawl on forearms toward my car. I would be okay if I could just get away.

"Are you seriously trying to crawl to your car?"

"I'll put some ice on it when I get home." I whimpered, trying to hold back the scream of agony that was mounting. I had never broken a bone before, but I was pretty sure that's what I'd done. This was the worst pain in the entire world.

"You're not going home. I'm bringing you to the ER," he said, trying to loop his arms under mine. I swatted him away.

"No, I can do it myself. I just need to get to the car." I tried inching along the sidewalk again, but the pain was too great.

Scott's face looked down at me, the fading sun creating a halo effect around him.

"Is accepting my help really worse than the pain you are in?" he asked. The hurt in his voice was clear.

"No, it's not that. It's just that I have already messed with your life enough as it is." I had screwed up everything. Every single thing I had tried to do in life had ended up like this: broken. Big, fat, ugly tears began to roll down my face. "Just leave me alone. I'm better off alone. I can only hurt myself if I'm alone."

Scott helped me to sit upright. "No one is better off alone, Julie."

"I'm not so sure about that."

Once my head stopped spinning, I figured I'd be able to hop in my car and drive off using my left foot. I could handle this on my own, just like I handled everything else in my life.

My plan was thwarted, however, when Scott scooped me up into his arms.

"Whoa, what are you doing? Put me down," I said, trying to resist.

He didn't even look at me as he took long strides toward his garage. "You can't walk on a broken ankle. You'll make it worse. You're going to the hospital."

"It's just a sprain," I said with no hope that I was right. "I'll be fine after some ice and painkillers."

"Julie. I'm a nurse. I think I know a break when I see one. Now shut up. You're going to the ER."

Seeing as there was little I could do to stop him, I let him carry me to his truck and fasten me in.

"You can just drop me off at the front entrance. I can manage from there."

Scott shook his head. "Sorry, Jules. You can't get rid of me that easy. We're not done talking yet."

I bit my lip. "And now you know why I was running in the first place."

Chapter 27

The X-ray rattled like plastic thunder in the doctor's hand as he entered the room to deliver my fate. From the stern look he gave me, I knew it was bad news. Then again, he looked like he had a tongue depressor shoved up his ass when he first examined my foot so maybe that was just his resting bitch face.

"Somebody's going to get a cast today," he announced, a slight semi-evil grin on his face. Dr. Andrews slid the X-ray into the viewing panel along the far wall with the grace of a gesture practiced a million times. He flicked on the light, and the black-and-white image of the inside of my foot was illuminated; the break was clearly visible even to the untrained eye.

"How long will she be the cast for?" Scott had read my mind and asked before I had a chance.

"At least six weeks, but more likely eight," he said nonchalantly.

"Eight weeks," I shrieked. I couldn't be in a cast eight weeks. I had to get out of town. How was I going to do that if I couldn't even walk, let alone drive? Leave it to me to break my driving foot.

The doctor ignored me and turned to Scott, the less hysterical one. "The break is clean, and shouldn't require surgery as long as she keeps pressure off the ankle."

Scott placed his hand gently on my good leg, as though to assure me, but he must have thought better of the gesture because he withdrew it a moment later. I wasn't sure what was more upsetting, the fact that his heart had told him to comfort me, or that his brain had instructed him to stop.

"We'll get her cast on and give you some written instructions, but she's going to need to take it easy, especially the first few weeks. Nurse Jacobs here can tell you that's when most patients take too many chances and end up having to come back in for surgery." His last comment was for my benefit. I knew it because he focused on me as if talking to a rebellious teen. He wasn't far off.

"Dr. Andrews is right. You need to give it time to heal."

Then the doctor glanced back at Scott. "She's going to need your help for awhile. Baby her."

My face turned red. "Um, no, actually we're not—"

"Of course, I'll take care of her," Scott said without skipping a beat.

The doctor glanced between the two of us, clearly uncomfortable that he had made some sort of faux pas, but quickly recovered with a rehearsed smile. "Well then, let's get this foot dressed, shall we?"

For the next hour or so a nurse came in with pain meds and my foot was washed, prepped, and wrapped with gauze. When the doctor took out a small white bucket with water. For a moment, I thought he might be baptizing my foot, but then he dipped a roll of blue material inside. He gave it a gentle squeeze and proceeded to wrap the wet blue layer of turned out to be plaster around my ankle and half way up my calf. All I could think the entire time was *thank God I shaved this morning.*

After I was sufficiently mummified, I was informed that the cast would harden in about fifteen minutes, but to be really careful with it with the first few days as the plaster could crack. I'd be put in a special boot I could walk on in a few weeks. Until then, I was stuck with crutches. *Awesome.*

"She'll be careful," Scott answered for me, watching the doctor intently go over the home care instructions.

We were discharged shortly after that, with a final note for me to follow up with my PCP in a week who could put the boot on for me. I didn't have a doc in New Hampshire, but I wasn't about to mention that. I would figure it out once I got home.

The entire day had turned into a disaster of epic proportions, and the last thing I wanted to think about was how I was going to pay for it all. As it was, the insurance card I'd given the lady at the desk was no longer in effect. I kept waiting for someone to come in, mid-wrap of the cast and kick me out for insurance fraud, but since we were in a small town and the people all thought I was a movie star, no one came to ask me to leave. Instead, the nurses had lingered in the hall, whispering to themselves and pointing at Scott, who he likely knew but didn't acknowledge. It was only a matter of time before this got out to the press. Cassandra was going to kill me.

I probably should have called her on the way to the ER. She could have arranged for payment, hell, she might have even been able to get a doctor to come out to the mansion, but I was just so embarrassed about the whole thing.

I listed Morgan's house as my home address on the insurance paperwork, so I knew a bill would find its way to me, eventually. Maybe by then, I would have the money I was owed. Or not. The bill would get paid. Eventually. I paid my debts. Just not always on time.

I couldn't think about that now. I still had to figure out a way to leave town.

Once Scott finally maneuvered me back into his truck, I tried to maintain my composure. A breakdown was imminent, I could feel it, and I didn't want to do it in front of him. Things would be okay…they would work themselves out, somehow. They always did.

Macy was in town, after all. I knew I could count on her to help me, but I also knew she would be occupied getting Morgan's memoir written and would be secretly ticked if I took her away from that. This was a huge project for her. Morgan was, by far, the biggest celebrity she'd ever covered. I couldn't ask her to leave that opportunity to care for me. Not that I had a place to go other than Morgan's. I knew she'd insist I stay with her while I recovered; so while it wasn't an ideal plan, at least there was someplace to go.

I didn't notice until we were on High Street, however, that we were going the wrong way.

"I think you missed the turn. The mansion is back there," I said, pointing my thumb behind us.

Scott adjusted his mirror but didn't make any attempt to turn around.

"I'm not taking you to the mansion. If what you said is true…if Morgan is really as sick as you say, you can't add to her burden. It sounds like she's got her medical care covered and people there to tend to her. She doesn't need the added stress right now. She needs rest."

"But…" Scott hit the blinker lever and pulled to a stop at the approaching red light.

"You can stay with me. I'll set you up in my room. It's on the first floor. I can sleep upstairs in the—"

"No, I can't ask you to do that," I said.

He turned to glance at me for a second. "You didn't ask. I offered."

"I know," I replied, getting flustered. "I just…I don't want you to feel obligated to take care of me simply because I fell while on your property. It's not as though I'm going to sue or anything. I'll figure something out. I could go to a hotel," I said, thinking out loud. "Morgan owes me money, so I could just—"

Scott glanced over at me, his eyes practically rolling out of his head. "You going to ask her to give you money while she's on her deathbed?"

Ugh, I'm an ass.

"I could crash at Cassandra's," I tried weakly.

"Would staying with me really be so bad?" His face fell.

"No, it's not that at all."

Scott smiled. "Well then, it's settled. You'll camp out with me until you're ready to leave."

What if I'm never ready? The second I thought that, I scolded myself. *Don't fool yourself, Jules. He's just being nice.* It's probably like a Hippocratic nurse's oath or some shit. Help the poor and decrepit, and all that crap.

"I'll be out of your hair as soon as I figure something out," I said. I hated how deflated the words sounded.

"Let's just get you home."

Home. Such a small word. The only problem was—I didn't have one. I hadn't had one since I left for college, and that never really seemed like home either. We moved so often, I never even committed our address to memory. It had never mattered before where I called home. Today, it was the only thing I craved.

When Scott pulled the truck into his garage, I unbuckled and reached for the door but was quickly scolded for the attempt. Apparently, I was not allowed to even open a door without help. His pampering me—however briefly it would last—was, well, nice.

It took about ten minutes to walk up two steps from the garage, hobble through his kitchen and into his living room before I was finally able to gently collapse onto the couch. The throbbing in my foot was intense from being down for so long. It was a relief to finally prop it up. The pain meds they had given me at the hospital were starting to wear off, and I was trying really hard not to complain about it. Even though the doc had written a prescription for more, I wouldn't be able to fill it. With no insurance, I couldn't pay the out-of-pocket expense. I knew I needed to get insurance, of course, but I sort of needed to get a job first. Until then, I'd just have to tough out the pain. There was no other option.

Despite my best attempts to hold the agony in, I grimaced when Scott placed the pillow under my foot. Thankfully, he didn't see it. He was right in his element, nursing me back to health. I was careful not to mistake his kindness for anything more than instinct.

"Okay. Anything I can get you before I go get your prescription?" said he asked, looking at me with slight concern.

"You don't have to do that," I said, trying to brush off his offer.

Scott frowned. "You planning on driving over to the pharmacy yourself?"

"Well, no I just meant I don't really need the meds."

"Um, yes, you do. I've seen you grimace no less than six times since we got here. You'll be due for more soon."

It was my turn to frown. "Yes, it hurts. I broke my ankle. Naturally, it will hurt, but I will be fine," I said through slightly gritted teeth as I tried to position my foot in a way it wouldn't throb so much. *Man, this hurt.*

Scott threw his hands up into the air. "Why won't you let me help you?" From his expression, it was clear he thought he was being personally affronted.

Sighing, I had to swallow my pride. I couldn't have Scott thinking this was about him. "I don't have insurance, all right? Now that Morgan's back, I don't even have a job. So, it's not that I don't want your help or the medicine, it's just that *I can't afford it*, okay?" The tone of my voice was far more hostile than it should have been.

"But I saw you give them an insurance card in the ER."

More confessions.

"That sort of expired…"

"Ah."

"Like five years ago."

Scott stared at me for a moment, not with the pity I expected, but more with a look of determination.

"In that case, you'll owe me."

Without another word, he left the house and was in the truck and backing out of the garage, completely ignoring my insistent shouting that I was fine.

Chapter 28

While Scott was gone, I tried to come up with a plan. I needed to find some way to dig myself out of the black pit I had fallen into. I knew I couldn't take advantage of his hospitality for long. My pride wouldn't allow it. I had to find a way to pay him back for everything he had done. This little trip to the ER was likely going to cost a large chunk of whatever I had made while pretending to be Morgan…if I managed to get anything at all.

While trying to brainstorm solutions, I realized that I should probably call Macy. It had been a several hours since I left the house to return Tripod, who was still bounding around happily from room to room, oblivious to the fact that I was now her human doppelganger.

Under normal circumstances, Macy would probably be worried that I hadn't returned promptly, considering I skipped town the last time she didn't hear from me; however, she may not have even noticed the time pass. She had a story to get and the rest of the world tended to fade away when she was on a deadline. Still, she should know where I was.

Bernard's car phone was still parked in front of Scott's house. A hop, skip, and a jump for a normal, able-bodied person. For me, it was like running a marathon or two.

I glanced around the room to see if Scott had a landline anywhere but saw none around me. I hadn't recalled seeing one in the kitchen when I went through, and the dining room wasn't a likely place to hold one either. This not having a cell phone thing was driving me insane.

Just then, I noticed a small area adjoining the living room that showed some potential. Craning my neck, I could see a tiny sliver of it through the open door. It might be an office. Surely, there would be a phone in there.

Since I'd never been very good at sitting idle, I opted to give it a shot. Reaching over to the chair beside me where the crutches were leaning, I tried, unsuccessfully, to snatch them. Naturally…they were out of my reach. Cursing, I swung my injured leg off the pillow and laid it gently on the ground until I was sitting upright. Intense throbbing in the ankle began almost immediately.

While grunting in pain, I reached for the closest crutch. In doing so, I knocked over the other one, and it crashed with a loud, reverberating *smack* against the hardwood floor. I managed to poke at the fallen crutch with the edge of my good foot until I was able to drag it within reach. By the time I had both of them in my hands, a small bead of sweat rolled down the back of my neck. This was going to be a long six weeks.

Being as careful as possible, so as not to make it an eight-week recovery, I pulled myself up to standing and inched my way toward the door on crutches, beyond annoyed that the underarm pads of the things literally did nothing to cushion my pits.

When I hit the bottom of the old wooden door with the rubber base of the crutch, it creaked out in protest before it revealed an office. I smiled at being right. Although it had the same dark wood paneling as the living room, the office was noticeably more peaceful, brighter than the rest of the house. A large bay window overlooked a line of trees bursting with fall colors. The faint top of a mountain peeked over the tallest of limbs as the last of the evening sun illuminated the room. It wasn't the killer view that made the office so different, though. The room felt special. Sacred somehow.

I studied the walls behind Scott's desk. The area was filled with dozens picture frames in varying sizes and colors.

In each, lived the face of a child or infant. I hobbled closer to the wall and saw that under each one was their name. I looked over the faces again. These must be the children he'd cared for, the children he had helped bring into the world. Lives he may have even helped save.

He was a *good* man. An honest man. I hadn't believed they still existed.

I looked a bit longer at the wall until my foot began to throb too much to keep standing. There had not been a phone in here, but there was a couch that was a lot closer than the one in the living room.

Sighing, I lowered myself onto the small white loveseat that overlooked the bay window. I laid my head back against the overstuffed arm and propped my foot on the other arm and closed my eyes. The couch was so soft. Almost like being held. I could see myself lying on this very couch curled up with Tripod on my lap as Scott flipped through one of his vast collection of books that were stacked on floor-to-ceiling shelves behind me. I could clearly picture him sitting there at his desk, his feet propped up as he leaned back in his chair…I swear I could even smell the cup of coffee steaming beside him. It would be so effortless being here…with him.

I smiled at the thought just as a soft cry emerged from the living room.

"I'm in here, Tripod."

A moment later, the kitten raced into the room, sniffed around a bit, and then jumped up onto the couch and curled her tiny body on top of my chest to sleep.

"That looks like a great idea, buddy," I whispered patting her soft orange fur. I closed my eyes along with hers, more than ready to drift off into the imaginary world I had begun to create. While my conscious mind knew it was Tripod resting on my chest, I pretended it was Scott head's there instead. His thick curls replaced Tripod's fuzz as my fingers stroked her grateful back. As I touched her fur, I envisioned Scott's body intertwined with mine as we slept the day away on some lazy afternoon. The cat's purr even seemed to call out my name. Ju—lie. Ju—lie. Ju—lie. The purr turned itself into the sound of Scott's voice. This dream was about to get good.

"Hmmm…Scott," I moaned in a husky, wanting tone.

"Um, everything okay?"

My eyes flew open to reveal a blushing Scott kneeling beside me, confirming that I had just moaned his name. Tripod jumped off my chest leaving me feeling cold.

"You okay?" he asked again.

"Yeah, I'm fine. I guess I nodded off." I said, praying I wasn't as red as he was.

Scott smiled. "Sorry to wake you, it sounded as if you had a good dream."

If I hadn't been blushing before, I was now. "It was, actually."

He sat in front of me on the coffee table next to the couch and set down a white paper bag. On the floor, I noticed a new litter box and a small suitcase which Tripod was examining.

"What's in the bag?" I asked, a sick feeling in my stomach.

"Your pain pills," he said.

I shook my head. "I meant the other bag. Are you going someplace?" I hated the level of panic that laced the question.

He gave me a small smirk. "No. I'm not going anywhere, and neither are you. That's yours." The confusion on my face must have been clear because he elaborated. "I knew it was going to take the pharmacy a while to fill your prescription, so after I got Tripod a litter box and some kitten food, I thought I'd stop by the mansion and let them know what happened."

"You spoke to Morgan?" I blanched.

"Yeah, the big guy didn't seem too happy about that."

"He probably didn't know that Morgan said I could tell you the truth." I winced.

"Well, he does now."

"Right."

Scott gestured to the bag. "Morgan insisted I bring you a bag with a few of your things."

"My things? But nothing there was really mine…"

He shrugged. "I was told there was a week's worth of clothes inside, so you must have had something."

Morgan had given me some of her clothes. Bless her.

"Thank you," I whispered, holding back emotion. Anthony would never have done something like that. He never would have thought of my needs. Never in a million years.

"How did she look?" I asked. What horrible timing this whole thing was. I should be there, helping to take care of her. Instead, I need help of my own.

He shrugged. "Morgan looked good, actually. She was sitting up, had color in her face, not as dire as I thought it may have been. No fever. I told her she was dehydrated. She needs IV fluids and something for the nausea probably wouldn't hurt. I advised her to get a doctor in there."

"I'm sure she's got one on speed-dial," I said but wondered if that was true.

"Your friend, Macy, didn't seem to like me," Scott said, laughing.

I made an apologetic face. "I would have warned you about her had I known you were going over there."

"I think she wanted to hurt me."

I shook my head. "No, not just you, basically all men who enter my life."

"Is she gay? Like, crushing on you?" Scott asked so sincerely that it made me laugh.

"No. She's as straight as they come." I let out a breath, feeling he was owed an explanation for what was sure to be a nasty round of a hundred questions from her. "You have to understand. Macy is my dearest friend, which means she knows me better than anyone. She has seen, firsthand, how painfully bad my judgment in all things is, especially when it comes to guys in my life." Scott's face shifted at the mention of him being a *guy in my life*. I held up a hand. "I didn't mean it like that, it's literally all guys: the mailman, waiters, the bus driver, any guy who crosses my path. Macy is there like a bulldog protecting me."

Scott frowned. "You can't take care of yourself?"

I laughed. It was a fair question. “Clearly, you don’t know my history.”

“No. I don’t. I know remarkably little about you, actually.”

It was true. What few details he knew of me had been a lie.

“Well, let’s just say if a guy paid any attention to me, I followed him around like a lost puppy.” I stared down, ashamed of my own behavior…and admitting it to Scott.

“I find that hard to believe,” he said, frowning.

“No. It’s true. Anthony was a prime example of that.” I shook my head. “I mean, the guy was married. Not happily, but still…married. And I stuck around.” I shook my head again. “I convinced myself that he *had* to pick me. He *had* to love me.” I swallowed hard. “*Somebody* had to,” I whispered, hopefully too softly for Scott to hear.

I batted away a tear that threatened to fall and smiled big.

“So, yeah, Macy was just looking out for me. Sorry.”

He nodded solemnly, as though he wanted to talk more about it, but opted to let it go.

Scott grabbed the paper bag and took out a few pills from the bottles beside him. I took the proffered medicine willingly from him, ready to swallow it down dry when he reached down into the bag and pulled out a bottle of water. I downed them, more than ready for the throbbing to return to the dull roar it had been in the hospital.

"You know," Scott began, "Bernard was giving me the stink eye too."

"Bernard?" I asked, raising an eyebrow. "What did he do?"

"Well," Scott said, scratching at the back of his head, "he didn't really *do* anything. It was more like the whole *overbearing father* thing going on. He said he didn't feel comfortable allowing you to stay with a man he didn't know." Scott cocked his head to the side. "They were all concerned about you. It seems as though, in the short time you've been here, you've affected quite a few people's lives."

I scoffed. "Oh, I've affected their lives, all right. I did what I always do: screwed things up."

Scott shifted his weight on the coffee table and peered into my eyes. He surprised me by taking my hand in his. "You don't think very highly of yourself, do you?" His voice was kind, but the question was a direct hit to my heart.

I bit my lower lip to keep it from quivering, but no voice would come, so I shook my head the smallest of increments before closing my eyes from the unplanned emotion that poured out of me.

A moment later, Scott was snuggled on the couch beside me, pulling my head onto his chest and whispering, "Everything is going to be okay, Jules. It's all going to be okay." It was such a simple sentence but one I had actually never been comforted with. *Would everything be okay?* I really wanted it to be. I wanted it to be okay with him.

Chapter 29

The sound of a large rumble caused my eyes to fly open. My first thought was earthquake. I wasn't shaking, though. The ground should be shaking if it was an earthquake. My panic decreased as I opened my eyes, squinting against the sunlight that flooded the room. I'd slept the night away on his couch. Guess I was tired.

I blinked a few times, wondering for a moment if I had dreamed the noise. Just then, the noise came again. It was a deep, scraping sound, like something being dragged against the ground outside.

"What the hell?"

I wanted to walk over to the window to investigate, but when I tried to reach for my crutches, I realized I needed another pain pill first. *Ow.*

As I reached for the bottle, a light rapping came on the door. Scott's head poked in. He smiled when our eyes met. It made my skin feel warm.

“Good morning, sleepyhead. I think those sleeping pills I gave you yesterday worked.” He grinned.

I rubbed my head. “Ugh, is that what I took?”

“You needed your rest. Today, you just get this one.” Scott gestured to a tray in his hand. It had a pill bottle in the center of it.

“Wonderful.”

“I brought you some coffee, too.”

Indeed, he had. He set down a small tray that held two cups, a bowl of sugar and a carton of Half and Half.

I lifted my hand against the light so I could see him better. “Oh, thank you.” I pushed up to a sitting position on the couch ignoring the throb in my foot. I was getting spoiled but couldn’t say I didn’t love it.

He handed me a pill and a cup, and I swallowed it down willingly.

The weird scraping sound came again.

“Hey, what’s that noise? Should we be evacuating or something?” I asked. Scott stopped to listen as though he hadn’t heard the noise.

“Oh, that’s just the plow guy. We got dumped on last night.”

“Dumped on? With what?”

He laughed. "Snow."

I blinked at him. "Snow? It's only the third of November!"

"Yeah? And?" His voice held no trace of humor. Was this a thing? *Did snow really happen before Thanksgiving up here? That seemed…Un-American!*

Scott grinned at me, unfazed by my inward horror. "They're predicting a good foot by afternoon." He walked over to the blinds and closed them, so I didn't have to squint anymore.

I blinked at him as my eyes adjusted to the new darkness. "Wait, a foot? A foot of snow?" The shock in my voice was evident.

Scott laughed. "Yeah. We're going to get slammed next week too, they say." He busied himself with fixing his own coffee as though the weather forecast was no big deal.

"What do we do? Who do we call? Do we have enough provisions to survive?"

He frowned. "Provisions? It's only snow. Jules." He put his mug down.

"Wow. Snow. The last time I saw snow, I must have been like four or five. We lived in Ohio for a few months. I don't really remember it. But I've seen pictures of me in a snowsuit, so I know I played in it." I chuckled. "I'll be damned. Never thought I be living in a place where I'd see snow again." I set my coffee down and tried to peer out through the cracks in blinds.

Without a word of preparation, Scott scooped me off the couch, blankets and all and carried me out of the office.

"Whoa, what the hell are you doing?" I asked, trying to will my body into weighing less than it did.

"I'm going to show you the snow," he said in a calming tone.

I laughed. "You could just open the blinds and let me see it that way, you know."

He shook his head. "Nah, you have got to feel it. Taste it. Be one with the snow."

"It's really okay," I tried. "I can watch it from the safety of the warm house."

Scott paused before opening the kitchen door. "There are two ways to experience life, Jules. You can either face the world or hide from it." His face grew serious. "It seems to me you've been playing it safe your whole life…just watching the world through the window."

I blinked up at him. My smile was gone at the truth in his words. I felt very small inside his arms just then. Exposed, somehow. "All I'm asking is that you at least see what's out there before you lock the door." He paused for a moment. "I can't make that choice for you. It *has* to be your call. Say the word, and I'll bring you back to the safety of your window seat."

His face was without humor as he waited for me to make up my mind. I glanced out the kitchen window toward the world beyond the threshold. Everything in sight was covered in a blanket of white. Small flakes continued to fall from the sky in a gentle, effortless way. It was all so white and positively stunning. It was new. Different. And somewhat terrifying.

"Well, do we go out or not?"

I hedged. I knew this was about more than just going out and seeing some damn snow. Scott was opening a bit of himself to me. An olive branch of sorts. I wasn't foolish enough to think he had forgiven me for all of the lies I had told, but it seemed as though he was asking me, via the snow, to take a chance. A chance on him? On us? On winter in general? That's what I wasn't sure of.

"How do you know I won't get hurt?" I asked. "I might slip and break my other leg. Or, what if you dropped me?

Then we could both get hurt." My heart raced with irrational thoughts at the weight of this metaphorical decision.

"I'm not going to drop you." He tightened his grip as though to reassure me. The gesture only made the panic worse.

"But, how do you know? It could be icy out there. You might not to mean to hurt me but maybe you will. Or maybe I'll end up hurting you." I knew I wasn't talking about the snow anymore, but I couldn't seem to stop myself.

He shifted me around to open the door with one hand. "I won't let you go, Julie. Not unless you ask me to."

I held my breath as the screen door opened, but Scott held me firmly inside, awaiting my call.

The air outside wafted over us. I was surprised it wasn't nearly as cold as I had anticipated. It was all so pretty to look at. I felt my breath catch while taking it all in. Small walls of snow encased the yard in peaks and valleys formed by gusts of wind. The massive trees surrounding his property were now weighted down with snow. It was so quiet…as though the snow had turned the volume of the world to mute.

I pulled my eyes away from the winter wonderland to gaze back into his waiting eyes.

“You won’t let me go?” I asked, far more timid than I had intended.

“I won’t let you get hurt again.” This time, there was no denying his meaning even if neither one of us could vocalize it. He wasn’t going anywhere.

“Julie?” he asked. It was still strange to hear him use my real name instead of Morgan’s. “I know I have no right to ask, and I might be reading this entire situation wrong, but I’m going to anyway.” He let out a small breath. “I would very much like to kiss you. Would that be okay?”

My eyes widened, and my heart began to beat faster.

“Only if you do it out there. In the snow.”

He raised an eyebrow. “Are you sure?”

I laughed. “No, but I’d like to see what the fuss is all about.”

He nodded once and stepped outside with me still in his arms. Scott stood there for a moment before he took one step closer to the edge of the porch to allow me to see the view better. In that single move, he promptly slipped. We were both on our butts a moment later.

“Shit, are you okay?” he asked inching across the icy porch on his elbows to check on me.

As I lay flat on my back, his face hovering over me, I began to laugh hysterically at the irony of it all. “Julie? Are you okay? Did I break something else?” The sudden panic in Scott’s voice made me smile.

“My butt hurts, but I think I’ll live.” He tried to inspect my limbs for any new injuries, but I reached up and brushed some snow off his face. I watched in awe as it melted instantly onto my skin.

His eyes closed with the gesture, opening slowly to gaze down at me.

“So, I guess I dropped you,” he confessed.

I smirked. “I noticed.” Shame crept onto his face, clearly embarrassed by his clumsiness. “But you know what? I’m going to get hurt sometimes. We both will.” I gave him a small smile. “It’s a good thing I have a nurse here to help me.”

I reached my hand out for his aid in standing back up, but he ignored it, staring at me.

“I will be, you know? For as long as you want me to be.”

I looked up at him, afraid I misunderstood his meaning. Unsure what to believe.

He brushed a strand of hair off my face. “That didn’t come out right. I guess what I’m saying is, I’d like to start over again. Get to know *you* as Julie." I lowered my head, but his hand brought my face back up to his. "I have a sneaking suspicion there was more of you in the role you were playing than of the movie star, and if that was the case…well, I liked *her*."

"I liked her, too," I admitted. "She was a tougher version of myself, I think.

"Well, then. Maybe we should try and figure out how Scott and Julie are together?"

I smiled. "I think I'd like that."

Before I could even wish for his lips to be on mine, they were. On the cold porch, getting dusted with snow, we lay there, kissing like a couple of teenagers. I'd forgotten what a good make-out session felt like. Anthony had never allowed time for foreplay. We were always racing against the clock. With Scott, it seemed as though there was nothing ahead of us but time.

How fantastically refreshing this all was.

Chapter 30

After we pulled apart from each other, a bit breathless from it all, Scott pulled what little blanket we weren't using over my shoulders and wrapped me into a tight embrace.

"Maybe we should head inside before we get frostbite?"

"Oh, God," I said, not even considering the fact I could lose a butt check out here. "Good plan."

Together, we scrambled on hands and knees to get back into the house as best we could because of the ice and my broken ankle and all. It wasn't exactly graceful, but it was full of giggles.

Once we were finally in the safety of his kitchen, Scott grabbed my hand and pulled me up to standing and said, "Why don't we go and warm up by the fire?"

He didn't wait for my answer but instead lifted me off my feet and over his shoulder in one swift motion. My tush was high in the air as his hands gripped against the back of my thighs as he carried me, caveman-style into the living room. Not gonna lie, it was hot as hell. As much as I wanted him to just drop me down onto the couch and ravish me, he was gentle with my broken body, laying me down delicately and tucking a throw around me before he cuddled up close.

This was so new to me. Sex had always followed the first kiss. The old me would have assumed Scott wasn't that into me because he hadn't brought me into his bedroom. This new Julie, however, knew it meant this relationship was going to be different. I was surprisingly okay with that.

We sat beside each other, my face resting against his shoulder, his hand running through my hair as we chatted about childhood memories, high school crushes and all the things we had screwed up in our lives. For hours, we shared everything and nothing, all at the same time.

I'd never talked with someone for that long, not even Macy. A few hours was about all I could take of her. She just had so much energy. After a while, I needed some quiet to recoup. But I didn't feel that with Scott. No matter what he said, I didn't tire of hearing his voice. The experience was such a deliciously foreign one.

The conversation wasn't one-sided either. Scott didn't speak to hear himself talk; he sincerely wanted to listen to my stories, too. I shared with him all of my battle scars. How I hated bouncing around from one place to another while my dad was in the Navy, how hurt I was when he left us, how I sometimes blamed myself for his leaving…For the first time, I felt heard, listened to.

His lips met the top of my head as I spoke, and his arms held me tighter just when I needed it. It was all so different from what I was used to.

"This is so weird."

"What's weird?" Scott asked. His fingers laced around my waist under the blanket we now shared, seemingly unwilling to let any distance come between us. The closeness confused me even more.

"I was just thinking how none of the other guys I've ever hung out with have done this." I was careful to say *hung out* and not *dated* as I wasn't really sure what was going on with us. It seemed like dating, but I had misinterpreted relationships before.

"Done what?" Scott asked, rubbing his thumb along the back of my hand.

"Um, cuddled, I guess?" My cheeks reddened.

The prickle of his chin as it rested on my shoulder felt oddly comforting. "Really?"

I shrugged. "Most of the time it's just dinner or a movie, never holding hands, mind you, and then back to one of our places for sex, and then after they'd go." I frowned. "I guess there wasn't time to just cuddle."

"Wait? Are you saying that after…they just got up and left?" he asked, unbelieving.

"Usually." I focused on our intertwined hands, realizing how stupid I was for allowing that pattern to keep happening.

"That is no way to treat someone you care about."

I nodded and turned to face him. "That's just it, though. I don't think any of them *did* care about me. Oh, sure, they wined and dined me, but once they got what they wanted…" I gazed down at my feet poking out of the blanket. "At first, that used to upset me. But then, I guess I got used to it. That was just how it was supposed to be, you know? All that after sex, cuddly glow stuff was like an urban legend or made-up shit or something. It didn't happen in real life." Scott remained quiet as the words spilled out of me. Something about this man made me feel safe enough to air my dirty laundry.

"When Anthony came along, though, I really needed to…I don't know…feel more than just a means to an end, for once. I wanted that intimacy I had only ever read about. I wanted someone to just hold me and ask nothing of me in return." The smile left my face and turned into a frown at my stupidity. "Our time was always so limited. A few stolen moments here or there when he could sneak away from his wife. I didn't want our time together to end, not because I loved him, really, but because I wanted so desperately to *be* loved." I let out a deep breath as the revelation of the moment washed over me.

Scott pulled my body closer to his. I let my back mold against his chest. I think I would miss this most of all when he finally left me.

"Do you think you're unworthy of love, Jules?"

And there it was. My one, ugly truth.

Tears I didn't even know had been building spilled down my face. "Yup," I sniffed. "I mean, look at me. I'm forty-two years old. Never been married, never been in a healthy relationship." I closed my eyes. "If it were going to happen, it would have by now, right?" Rivers of tears streamed down my face.

This is why you hold stuff in. This is why you don't let people get close to you. It hurts too damn much when they do.

He latched his hands tight around my waist. “Well, I think the answer to why you’re not married is pretty simple, actually.”

I snorted through my tears. “Oh, yeah? Why is that?”

His lips pressed softly against the nape of my neck, sending tingles down to my toes.

“You had to wait this long because you hadn’t met me yet.”

I turned my head over to catch the lie in the line he was feeding me, but I was shocked to discover I could only find sincerity.

“Oh, that was smooth.” I laughed.

“It’s also the truth.” He placed a gentle kiss on my lips, which led to another wonderfully long make-out session.

The sky turned dark as the day turned into night. We nestled in his living room, a blanket draped over both of our knees, empty Chinese cartons from the take-out he’d ordered earlier littered on the coffee table. The fire popped and hissed to its own erratic rhythm making us oblivious to the dropping temperatures outside. This was what heaven must be like.

I shifted on the couch and noticed something I hadn’t seen before on the end table. My cell phone.

“Hey, you got my phone!” I shrieked.

"Oh, yeah. When I got your stuff, Bernard gave it to me. He said he trusts you not to blow Morgan's cover."

I picked up the phone and removed the charging cord and held it in my hands. I quickly unlocked it and saw that I had no less than 2967 notifications, 98 emails, and about 300 missed calls. I didn't check to see who they were from because, honestly, I didn't want to see Anthony's name. Just thinking about him made me sick to my stomach.

There was only one person I had to call: my mom. She probably had a search warrant out for me by now. Although we weren't extremely close, we did chat on the phone about once a month or so. She probably thought I was blowing her off, which, I sort of was. Though, to be fair, my phone had been taken hostage.

"I gotta call my mom." I sighed.

"Okay. I'll give you some privacy. I'm sure I have some emails of my own to answer. I got a bit distracted today." He flashed a wicked grin before getting up to go to his office.

"What do I tell her?" I asked. "I can't tell her the truth…I'm still not at liberty to talk about Morgan."

He stopped, walked behind me and rubbed my shoulders. "Then tell her everything else. Tell her you moved out of the city because you knew the man of your dreams lived in Bucksville, New Hampshire."

I snorted. "Yeah. That'll work." Scott left me feeling all warm and fuzzy. He'd just referred to himself as *the man of my dreams*. I was oddly okay with that.

Chapter 31

It took an hour, but I finally convinced my mom that I was alive and well and didn't need her to fly out from Florida to come get me. Once she got over her anger for not telling her where I was, we had a long talk about the time she ran away from home when she was seventeen. It turned out that my mother was a pretty naughty girl in her day, so she was probably more forgiving because her daughter had, at least, waited until she was in her forties to run away from home.

When I hung up, I knew Macy would be next. I texted her first, though. Waking a sleeping Macy with a phone call was never a good idea.

Let me know when you're up.

A moment later, she texted back.

Get your ass to Morgan's. ASAP.

I tried to text her back, but she didn't answer.

My stomach sank. *Morgan.* She must have gotten worse…or maybe…no, Macy would have told me if she'd died. *Wouldn't she?*

In full panic mode, I ignored my crutches and hopped over to Scott's office.

"We gotta go!" I shouted when I was halfway there.

He came rushing out. "What's wrong? Is it your foot?"

I shook my head. "No, but we need to go. Now. I think it's Morgan. Macy said we needed to get there fast."

He nodded once before helping me toward the garage. After Scott got me into his truck and lifted the garage door, I gasped.

"The snow! How are we going to get there in the snow?"

Scott gawked at me, seemingly amused at my ignorance. "Jules, my truck has four-wheel drive. We'll get there. Assuming someone's plowed Morgan's driveway."

"And if they haven't?" I asked.

"Well, then we'll be hoofing it up to the house."

I recalled the very long, very steep private road to her house. I frowned, looking down at my cast. "That would suck hard."

Scott reached over and touched my knee, giving it a gentle squeeze. “I’ll get you to her, Jules, even if I have to carry you.”

I smiled at him, realizing that was exactly what he’d do if necessary.

“Let’s hope it doesn’t come to that.”

While the drive there was slower than normal and nerve-wracking for me, we got to the mansion within ten minutes.

Mercifully, the driveway had been expertly plowed. Obviously, Morgan would have had a plow guy. She had staff for everything. Hell, she even hired someone to play *her*. That was the power of money.

The passenger door was open, and Scott was helping me out before I had even got the crutches in hand. Together, we bumbled up the steps where the door flew open just as we were about to knock.

It was Bernard. He had been crying. My heart sunk.

“What happened…is she?” I could feel myself grow pale. Instinctively, I reached out for something to hold onto. I was shocked when Scott’s hand found mine.

“She’s…getting better.” Bernard cried. “The doc is here. He thinks she’s taken a turn.”

I glanced behind him and noticed there was, indeed, a doctor sitting on the couch with Morgan. He was talking to her in a hushed tone as Cassandra paced behind the couch, biting her nails and hanging onto his words.

Macy rushed up to ask about my foot. I gave her the short version, far more interested in trying to get a grip on the turn of events here.

She must have seen my attention focused on Morgan and the IV stand at her side because she stopped her barrage of questions.

“We’ll exchange stories later,” she whispered, watching Cassandra approach the doctor.

I thunked my way into the living room with my crutches. I was fully aware of the hand Scott had pressed against my spine, helping me into the room. It seemed odd for someone to have my back as it were…odd in a good way.

At my noisy arrival, the doctor glanced up. “Miss Malone, I thought we agreed that visitors at this stage of your recovery was not wise.”

Scott took an inadvertent step back as though afraid he might be contaminating the air.

The doctor took a more serious look at me and gasped. “Oh, my. Is this her? Your doppelganger?” It was clear from the shock on his face that he thought I was a dead ringer for his patient.

Morgan smiled. “Mr. Yin, meet Julie Green.”

Mr. Yin stood up to get a closer angle.

“Remarkable. You *do* look just like her.”

“Well, to be fair,” Macy piped up from her spot at the edge of the room, “Morgan looks like Julie. Julie had that face first. You copied *her*.”

His eyes crinkled in delight when he addressed Macy. “Well, I didn’t perform that surgery myself. Some colleagues of mine did, still”—he turned back to me—“it’s remarkable.”

“Yeah, her recovery is too,” I said, trying to change the subject. “So, is she all better now?”

The doctor gestured for me to sit, noticing the fact that I was lame.

“She is showing signs of the treatment working, but we must be vigilant now more than ever. She must not exert herself or go outside. Her risk of exposure to illnesses is too great. No further company. Her immune system is still quite fragile.”

Macy and I exchanged a worried glance while Cassandra seemed annoyed by the extra work.

"Do you have masks?" Scott asked. "We could wear them?"

Mr. Yin nodded and brought out a box and placed a handful on the coffee table next to a bunch of other medical supplies. "I would prefer, however, to move her into the other room, to limit her exposure even more. Those coming into her room should wear gloves and a mask. At least until her white count is back to normal. I know it's much improved already, but I'm just being cautious." At that, he faced Morgan who gave him a small sigh of resignation.

Bernard put on a mask and scooped his beloved up into his arms. His hands were already covered with gloves, but he paused when he realized Morgan was still attached to the IV.

"Allow me." Scott slipped past me, grabbed some gloves from the box on the table, slapped on a mask and expertly detached the IV from a piece that connected her to the tubing.

It was sort of thrilling to see Scott getting in there, performing tasks he could probably do in his sleep. Still, it was sexy, somehow. That level of knowledge and confidence.

"Looks like her bag is almost done. Does she need another liter?" Scott asked.

Mr. Yin's eyebrows raised in question. "On your staff, is he?" He directed his question to Morgan.

“I’m not on her payroll, but I am a nurse who would like to offer some help, if you’ll take it,” Scott said with authority.

“Well, in that case, yes. I would like her to have another bag. I’ve given her some Zofran for the nausea so that issue should right itself.”

Scott nodded and accepted the bag Mr. Yin offered him from the depths of his black medical bag. He gave me a quick look before wheeling the IV stand after Bernard who had already left to bring Morgan into her room.

“I’ll check in on her tomorrow. For now, she needs as much sleep as possible,” Dr. Yin told the rest of us. “Keep visits short and hands and mouths covered. Call me if anything changes.”

With that, he gathered his things and left us to deal with the new reality.

Chapter 32

For the first several minutes, none of us spoke. It was almost as if we said anything, the spell that was making Morgan feel better might be broken.

Cassandra paced around before grabbing a mask and gloves, huffing as she put them on before she went to check on Morgan.

When the sound of her heels faded, Macy let out a breath.

"So, crazy, huh?" she said, walking over to the couch and plopping down. Her notepad was in her hands, and a lot of writing filled the pages.

"This will be great for the book."

Macy nodded solemnly. "It really will. Does it make me a horrible person for thinking that?"

I shrugged, "If it does, I guess we're both going to hell."

"It was the wildest thing. Bernard called Dr. Yin's office because he got all worried about what Scott had said about

Morgan being dehydrated. I mean, it was pretty scary for awhile there. I literally thought she was seconds away from dying. Dr. Yin rushed over, gave her the anti-nausea meds and the fluids, and she really started to bounce back. Dr. Yin was really angry that the hospital let her leave, but Bernard just told him, 'You clearly don't know Morgan. When she wants something, it happens. And she wanted out of that place,'" Macy explained. "Everything was happening all at once, and then you weren't here, and I just felt like I was in the way…but I also really wanted to be able to document the whole situation. I tried to stand in the shadows and just observe, but the whole thing was so surreal."

"I bet."

"When that guy came to let us know what happened to your foot, I almost tackled him thinking he had hurt you, you know, as if he'd shoved you down the stairs or something."

I laughed. "Ah, no. Just my own idiot self thinking I was far more agile than I am." I shifted my foot on the couch and rubbed at my head.

Cassandra came back in. Her hands were on her hips.

"Well, I just got a call from Dr. Yin. No one can leave the house."

"What? Why?" Macy and I said over each other.

"The paparazzi are staked out at the entrance. He said he barely got through. They know something is going on. Vultures."

"We didn't see anyone when we came in," I said.

Cassandra frowned at me. "They probably saw you. I can imagine the stories they must be coming up with. You and the nurse. Again." Her voice was agitated.

"Who cares—" I began to rant.

"Who cares? This is Morgan's *career* you're messing with. She has a boyfriend," she said, making air quotes over the word boyfriend. Cassandra collapsed into a heap on the couch across from us. Her long legs jutted out at odd angles. Her former perfect demeanor all but gone.

I was in too much pain to argue with where her priorities were, so I just laid my head back against the couch. I had no problem hanging out here as long as I didn't have to move my foot ever again. The adrenaline of the ride over had worn off, and my body was now punishing me for standing so long. I had no idea how Scott would react to a forced containment, however.

"Hold up," Macy said. "Are you telling me we can't leave? I have a job to get back to."

"Oh, don't be daft. It's not forever," Cassandra moaned. "Just until the gaggle of reporters leave. If they camp out too long, I can get the chopper to come by and remove us."

I looked at Macy and laughed. "The chopper. She thinks we're getting in a chopper." We both hated flying.

"When my notes are done, I'll get to the publishing house any way I can. I can close my eyes and just imagine we're driving," Macy said. With that, she went back to her notes and began scribbling.

"Okay," Scott said, coming into the room. His mask was resting below his chin as he pulled off the gloves in a swift, inside-out motion.

Cassandra sat up and tried to compose herself. "How is she doing?"

"She seems to be resting comfortably. I gave her my cell number if she needs anything. I don't need to be anywhere until tomorrow morning so I can be on call tonight." He tapped my shoulder. "We should probably leave and give her some time to rest."

"Ah, if only we could. We're trapped here." I said, resting my head back against the couch.

Cassandra took over at that point and relayed the bad news of our lockdown. Instead of being annoyed or indignant,

Scott sat down beside me and said, “Cool. I’ve never been to a slumber party.”

And a slumber party is exactly what it turned out to be. Cassandra was able to leave with no issues since she came and went all the time. She would just as soon run over the paparazzi as answer their questions, so she left around eight o’clock when she was sure Morgan wasn’t going to die on her. Once past the gate, Cassandra called to say there were still a half dozen of them perched out, even in the snow, but she thought they’d bow out when temps dropped below freezing overnight. None of us were keen on the idea of a midnight escape and opted to hunker down and see what the morning brought.

Macy and I took the spare bedroom on the first floor and Scott, ever the gentleman, offered to take the pull-out couch in the upstairs screening room.

Bernard stayed with Morgan the rest of the night, only coming out to get them something to eat or drink. His spirits were high now that she seemed to be on the mend. I’d never seen him smile so much. It warmed my heart.

Before the remaining three of us turned in for the night, however, we found some popcorn to snack on and proceeded to binge-watch the movies we had rented for Morgan last night. One of the previews was for a film Morgan was in.

"You know," Scott said, careful to speak softly since Macy had fallen asleep at some point, "I realize you told me that Morgan looked like you, but until I saw her up close today, I had no idea just how much you really do. It's uncanny."

I snuggled into his chest. He was so warm and soft, and I was more than content to fall asleep right there in his arms. It was exciting to be this close to him and know this was all it needed to be. He hadn't ever pushed for anything more.

"Mmm," I murmured. "It's amazing what plastic surgeons can do. Try not to confuse us, though, 'cause that would be awkward."

"Not a chance." He kissed the top of my head softly. "I will say, when I first walked in and saw her on the couch, all hooked up and stuff—I got scared."

I looked up at him. "Yeah, it's a pretty terrifying thing Morgan's going through."

He shook his head. "No, it's not that, it's just, well, I didn't see Morgan Malone on the couch at first. I saw you. It sort of wigged me out thinking for a split second that it was you who was sick."

"Oh," I whispered.

"Yeah. I didn't like it." His expression was troubled.

I reached up and touched his face. His hand met mine, and he pressed his cheek firmly against my hand.

"Hey, it's okay," I whispered. "I'm fine. Fit as a fiddle. Well, except for my foot, but that will heal."

He nodded but didn't say anything else. His eyes went back to the movie, but I could tell his mind was a million miles away, lost in some thought he wasn't about to share with me.

Chapter 33

When I awoke the next morning, it was not to the warmth of Scott's chest but to a crisp, white down pillow.

Squinting against the morning sun, I raised my head, searching for Scott, or at the very least, my bunkmate, Macy. Alas, I was in the room alone. I didn't recall coming to bed, so Scott must have carried me to my room. I wish I would have remembered that. I shifted onto my back and winced in pain. Stupid foot.

On the bedside table were my bottle of pills and a glass of water. I smiled. That little angel thought of everything. I lay in bed a moment until the pills kicked in, and then I grabbed the crutches, neatly leaned against the bed, and worked my way out of the room to find something to eat.

When I got into the living room, I found Scott there, sprawled on the small love seat, an end table pulled closer to support his feet. The small cashmere throw from the chair was the only thing covering his upper body. The poor guy looked so uncomfortable, but I didn't want to wake him. He'd likely had a hard time falling asleep as it was.

If he'd stayed in the living room, Macy must have gone upstairs to the screening room. Since there was no way I was going to make it up there without causing a ruckus, I hobbled into the kitchen in search of a quick snack.

When I got there, I was surprised to see Morgan sitting at the island, munching on some ice cream straight from the carton.

"Morning," I said quietly, flopping onto one of the bar stools. A bowl of fruit was centered on the counter, so I grabbed a handful of grapes as Morgan continued with her ice cream. She seemed lost in thought, and I didn't want to disturb her.

After a moment, she put down her spoon. "My God. I haven't had ice cream in years."

"Really?"

She smiled, a look of a contented sugar high on her face. "Nope. Not since the tabloids got a shot of me in a bikini. 'Cellulite City,' they said." She sighed. "Cassandra had hooked me up with a personal trainer and a new chef the next day." Morgan seemed really sad at the memory.

"I can't imagine the pressure that's on you to be, well, perfect." I put the grapes down, suddenly not hungry.

She shrugged. "That was the old me. I think this new me…if I'm lucky enough to live through this, is going to be more independent. If I want to eat ice cream, I'm going to eat ice cream, dammit. It's not as though I need the money anymore. I've got enough to be comfortable for the rest of my life. I don't care what people think about me now. Not since…"

"Not since getting sick?"

She focused on the counter. "Not since meeting Bernard." When her eyes raised to meet mine, they were bright, and her face glowed. "I know he seems like my complete opposite, but he sees *me*, you know? He sees me. The real me and he still loves me for it. I know now that's pretty damn rare, and I'm not going to live my life, what's left of it, for anyone else anymore. It's time I do what *I* want for a change." Her jaw was firm.

"I think that's wonderful. I really do." I beamed, even if I was a bit jealous of her determination. "Does Cassandra know about this change of heart?"

She laughed. "Not yet."

"I wish you luck with that conversation."

"Thanks."

We sat in silence for a few more moments. I went back to eating my grapes until Morgan offered me a spoon to share her ice cream.

"I wanted to thank you for helping me, Julie," she said. "Not many people would be willing to put their life on hold to help a perfect stranger."

I shrugged. "Well, to be fair, you *are* paying me."

She smirked. "Still, it was kind of you. I know it couldn't have been easy."

"There are worse things than pretending to be a movie star," I countered, "but, you're welcome."

She squeezed my hand.

"Well, I better get back. Bernard will flip if he wakes up and sees I'm not in bed, and worse, talking to someone outside of my confinement area." She giggled.

I finished off the ice cream she left. About half an hour later, Scott joined me in the kitchen.

"Morning," he said, scratching at the back of his head. "Sleep okay?"

"I'm going to say I slept better than you did." I shifted my foot on the stool beside me. "You didn't need to carry me to bed," I said, slightly embarrassed.

He grinned. “I like taking care of you. It’s fun. Besides, you talk in your sleep.”

At that, my head whipped up. “I do? What did I say?”

His smile grew wider. “My name.”

My cheeks blazed red.

“I did?”

“Maybe you did, or maybe I’m just messing with you. I’ll never tell.”

With that, he started rummaging around in the fridge.

“How about we make breakfast for everyone.” He shut the door, his arms full of eggs, bacon, and orange juice.

“Um, Morgan and I had some ice cream.”

Scott frowned. “All the more reason to eat a decent breakfast. Come on, you can crack the eggs.”

The day passed in a gloriously lazy fashion. We got reports that a few paparazzi were still lingering, so Scott canceled his CPR class to stay secluded with us. He said no one would have come anyway due to the snow. I was glad he didn’t need to leave. I wanted him there with me. We were a discombobulated family, but we had all united to rally around Morgan and to protect her and her secret.

Eventually, the paparazzi got tired or cold and left. The helicopter wasn’t needed, much to Scott’s dismay.

The next few days played out, one after another in quiet fashion. Little by little, Morgan got stronger as I made a few more brief appearances in town to subdue the paparazzi who loved the new boot Dr. Yin managed to obtain for me. I wasn't complaining, though. The boot allowed me to walk without crutches, which helped my way of life tremendously. Having that small amount of independence also made me far less needy.

Not that Scott stopped babying me. It was tricky to hang out with him because I couldn't exactly be seen in public with him, not while I was still pretending to be Morgan. He came to the mansion in his nurse scrubs under the guise of checking up not only on me but on my sick friend.

The tabloids were starting to make up all sorts of bizarre stories about this mysterious sick friend, so we opted to kill her off. Cassandra even hired a fake ambulance and volunteered herself to ride in the body bag out of the house. That was a kick.

We'd need to plan a fake funeral, too, I supposed, but for now, it seemed to get the photographers off our backs.

I could feel my time as Morgan was soon coming to a close as she grew stronger and stronger.

Macy flew back and forth a few times working on the last of her notes for the autobiography, pausing only long enough to poke fun at Scott when he showed up for to visit. She had come to like him, which was surprising to discover.

One night, while Scott was tucked away in the kitchen at the mansion making us all a lunch that consisted of nothing more than the Cheez Doodles and chocolate milk I had been planning on, I heard myself sigh.

"What's wrong?" Macy asked, raising her nose up out of her notebook. Even in that one sigh, she knew something was off with me. Good friends noticed those moments. Best friends pointed them out to you.

"Nothing," I hedged.

"Bullshit." She crossed her arms over her chest, which meant she was settling in for a fight if I didn't start talking.

"It's just that you have this wonderful new path with the book…It's gonna be huge, Macy, I can just feel it. And Morgan is on the mend so—"

"Where does that leave you?" she finished for me.

I studied my hands as if searching for the answer etched inside the lines. "I'm not sure why it should bother me so much. I mean, hell, I'm used to leaving jobs. It's what I do, but this one…this town…felt special." My eyes shifted back toward the kitchen for a moment. Macy followed my stolen glance.

"Oh, I see. This is about *the guy*."

I whipped my head back. "No, it's not about Scott," I tried to say in a convincing way. I failed miserably. "This town just seems, I don't know, like home. The idea of leaving here—"

Macy frowned. "Why do you have to leave?"

This conversation was making me frustrated, so I stood up and thunked over to the window, far away from the earshot of the kitchen. Macy followed after me. Her gold wrist bangles jingling as her short strides caught up to mine. I lowered my head to whisper. "I don't belong here. Now that Morgan is better, I'm not needed anymore."

Macy's face shifted from her snarky frown into a sternness she reserved only for me when she was about to lecture me about being ridiculous.

"All right, this pity party for one ends now."

I tried to roll my eyes and walk away, but her hand flew up and latched onto my elbow, holding me in place. While Macy had always been a spitfire, she had never pulled something like this. "No, Jules. You don't get to run away.

Not this time. You need to pull up those big girl panties and go after what you want."

I scoffed. "I don't know what I want."

Macy cocked her head up at me. "Are you for real? Are you seriously trying to stand here and tell me, your best friend, that you don't know what you want? Everyone in this damn house knows what you want." I averted her gaze while trying to mask my confusion. "We all have eyes, Julie. It doesn't take a rocket scientist to see that you want the dude in the kitchen."

I huffed. "You know what?" Macy shifted her weight to the side, ready to lay into me for being an idiot yet again. "You're right."

Her perfectly shaped eyebrows shot to the sky. "I am?"

I smiled. "Yes. It's time I make my claim."

At that, she hugged me hard and literally danced me around in a circle. "That's my girl. Go get your man!"

Using the fire that Macy lit under my ass, I marched, noisily, into the kitchen where Bernard was putting the final touches on a small tray of cheese and fruit for Morgan. She couldn't eat much at a time, so Bernard made her several small snacks a day. It was really sweet. Scott was busy chopping up salad to go with the sandwiches he'd made for the rest of us.

"Bernard, would you mind if I spoke with Scott in private for a moment?"

He and Bernard exchanged a *dude, you're in trouble* glance.

"Not at all," he said. "I was just about to bring this to Morgan anyway." He snatched the tray and started out of the kitchen without another word.

Scott gave me a curious look but gestured for me to continue.

"So, I've been thinking," I said, limping farther into the room but keeping a healthy distance from him.

"Yes?" Scott asked tentatively.

I began playing with the hem of my shirt.

"You're nervous," Scott said.

I looked up at him. "No, I'm not."

He motioned to my hands that were still on my shirt.

"Yes, you are. You fiddle when you're nervous."

I dropped the fabric and dragged my teeth over my bottom lip.

"Now, you're embarrassed."

I wasn't sure how to react at his observations. It was one thing for Macy to know my tells, but no guy had ever picked up on them before. The realization was both unnerving and soothing at the same time.

"Yes, fine, I'm nervous and embarrassed. I don't know how to tell you this, so I'm just going to come out and say it."

The playfulness left Scott's face and was replaced with what I could only describe as concern.

"What's going on, Jules? You're scaring me."

I let out a long breath. I wasn't sure I had the strength to do this. What if he wasn't on the same page? What if I was just a fling for him? What if I had read yet another man wrong?

"I was just talking to Macy."

"Okay…"

"She basically told me to shit or get off the pot," I blurted out.

Scott's eyebrows pulled together. "I'm not sure what you're getting at."

I moved past him, deeper into the kitchen and hid behind the island. I grabbed the side of the marble countertop for strength.

"I knew I wouldn't say any of this properly I don't know what I'm doing. Okay. Here's the thing. I've been a goddamn Goldilocks my whole lame life."

"Goldilocks? Like the children's story?"

I nodded. "Yes. Always searching for some place, some job, some*one* to feel just right." Scott took a step closer at that, but I held up a finger to stop him. Scott raised his hands briefly in surrender and waited for me to continue.

"I wasn't anticipating this small town in the middle of the boonies to be that place. I mean, there is still a foot of snow outside! Who lives in a place where there is a foot of snow on the ground? Only crazy people." I threw my hands up in the air and noticed Scott's face had turned from concerned to slightly amused at my increasing level of hysteria.

"And it's not as though the people here have been exactly welcoming, even when they thought I was a movie star."

"Surely, at least one or two of us have been kind to you?" Scott suggested.

My cheeks flamed. I started using a fingernail to clean a spot on the counter that wasn't really dirty. "There has been. Which brings me to my next point. I really like this town and some of the people in it." I could sense myself shriveling from embarrassment. "It will be a matter of weeks, days maybe, before Morgan is completely better, and then I won't have to pretend to be her anymore."

"So?"

"So, that means I have to start thinking about a new job."

"Okay…" Scott said, clearly not following my erratic path of logic. I didn't even know where I was going with this.

Deep breathes, Jules.

"The big question I have for myself is, do I search for a job here in Just-right-ville or do I head to a city where jobs I'm qualified for will actually exist?"

"Ah. I see." Scott walked over to the other side of the island and stood across from me, willing my eyes to meet his.

"Do you?" I asked.

"You want to know if what the two of us have is something permanent. Something solid. Something worth setting down roots for. Is that about the gist of it?"

I looked up at him…astonished he had actually understood the real question in that train wreck of a dilemma I faced.

Swallowing down the fear of what his answer might be, I nodded once.

He grabbed both of my hands.

"Jules, I would go down on bended knee right here if I thought that would convince you of the level of permanency I already consider us having." My eyes just about bugged out of my head at that. "I'm all in, Jules. I never thought I could feel this way again. After my divorce…well, let's just say I became quite bitter for several years. I had a really hard time with trust, as you clearly have seen. But when I met you, it was like rediscovering the person I used to be. I found myself actually smiling again." He wouldn't let my gaze leave his. "I know we just started seeing each other, but—"

Oh, the dreaded *but*.

"But if you want to leave…if you don't want this relationship to go any further than today, I will be devastated, but I will always be grateful to you for showing me the side of myself I had forgotten."

I blinked up at him through big fat tears that had welled.

Scott traced the pad of his thumb under my eye, catching the tear before it fell. He cradled my head in his hands, tilting my face upward to force my focus on him.

"What happens beyond this moment is entirely up to you, Jules. If you want to stay here, and if you want to stay with me…I would be the happiest man on earth."

I wanted to believe him, I really did.

"However," he went on, "if you don't feel the same way as I do, then perhaps you *should* move, or I should." His face fell. "Because I don't think I'm strong enough to live in the same town as you if you weren't with me."

I was quiet for a moment, taking it all in, willing myself to believe him, but a cloud of doubt still hung over me. After all, I had been fooled by poetic words so many times before. I had to protect my heart.

"I can't believe you pulled out the marriage card," I said, feeling my insecurities bubble to the surface. Anthony had dangled that same carrot. Over and over. "That's not the sort of offer you should make to a girl at this stage of the game." I blinked up at him, my eyes glazed over with too many emotions. "It's an empty promise."

Instead of getting defensive, as I assumed he would, he bent down on one knee.

"Oh. My. God!" Macy shrieked from the entryway, an empty teacup in her hands. "Is he seriously proposing to you right now?"

Scott grinned but kept his eyes on me.

"I was trying to," he said.

"You were?" Macy and I said at the same time.

"Morgan! Bernard, Cassandra, get your skinny asses in here. Scott's about to propose to Jules!" Macy bellowed.

My heart pounded in my ears, and I couldn't hear all the shrieks that came from the crowd who gathered around the kitchen island.

"Everyone, shut up," Morgan's voice echoed off the tile. "Let the man ask his question."

"No. He doesn't have to ask me anything," I said, coming back to my senses. "This was just a joke. He was just kidding. Trying to prove a point." I stared down at Scott whose face showed no indication of a bluff. "Weren't you?" My voice came out in a raspy whisper.

His hands tightened around my left hand. "I have never been more serious about anything in my whole life. You have restarted my heart, Jules. You brought me back to life, and you didn't even realize it."

I trembled at his words. This was actually happening. He was really asking me to marry him. I had no idea what I was going to say. Everything that had happened since I'd arrived in town had been a whirlwind. How could either one of us be sure that what we were feeling could stand the test of time? Marriage didn't guarantee a happily ever after. It hadn't worked with my parents or Macy's folk. Hell, I knew fewer people who were married than were divorced!

"I have always been a rational thinking man, Julie. I never took chances, never risked anything. Never asked for a promotion, never became the doctor I knew I could have been. I stayed where it was comfortable. Just like you, Jules. But when I'm with you, I feel like taking chances, discovering new things, as long as I get to do it with you. I'm putting it all on the line here, Jules. I'm asking you to risk a life with me." He cleared his throat. "Julie Green, would you do me the supreme honor of being my wife?"

I heard the collective intake of the breaths everyone made as they waited for my answer. Any attempts to stall for time were all used up. Scott was waiting, staring up at me with his big, silver eyes willing me to say yes.

But this wasn't what he wanted. Not really. He got caught up in the moment. He hadn't thought this through.

"Girl, if you don't say yes to this man, I'm gonna take you outside and kick the living shit out of you," Macy said, breaking the silence.

I kept my eyes on Scott but directed my response to Macy. "He has no idea how big a screw-up I am, Macy. He will regret his impulsiveness. Once he sees me for the disaster

I really am, it will be too late. He'll be stuck with a wife he doesn't want." I studied his face, the one that was ready to protest. "And I care for him too much to let that happen."

At that, I pulled my hand out of his grasp and hobbled as fast as I could out of the kitchen and out the front door. It was time to run again. This time…for good.

Chapter 34

A string of curse words erupted from my mouth as I tried to maneuver the porch stairs with the stupid boot. I didn't have on a coat or shoes, but it didn't matter. I had to leave.

I was angry. Angry that my damned foot was broken and I couldn't go faster, angry that Scott had put me in this position, angry that this godforsaken snow was going to prevent me from getting far, but mostly I was pissed at myself for refusing him. I knew I was never going to find anyone like Scott again. Perhaps, that was why I'd turned him down.

If I had said yes I would have risked becoming attached and latching onto something that wasn't permanent. I would have been setting my heart up for impending obliteration. History had taught me one thing: Men don't stay. Being alone was the only logical choice.

I had only barely cleared his truck when I heard Scott shout my name from the house. In my haste to go faster, I ended up slipping and falling straight on my ass. *Naturally.* The world hated me.

Humiliated beyond belief, I lost it. I was practically hiccupping the tears back by the time Scott reached me, easily scooping me up in one fell swoop into his arms.

"No, I can't go back in there. I'm too embarrassed!" I wailed.

Scott honored my wishes and instead carried me to his truck, where he managed to jimmy open the door and set me gently inside. He yanked a blanket from the back of his cab and threw it over my shivering limbs. A moment later, he was in the truck with me, warming my hands with his own. He dug out the keys from his pocket and started the truck, turning the heat up to high. The initial cool blast made me shiver deeper into the blanket.

"I'm sorry," Scott said after several long moments had passed.

I looked up at him, sniffing. "What are you sorry for? I'm the one who ran out." I felt so ashamed, admitting it out loud.

"True. But I'm the one who made you run. I shouldn't have asked you to marry me in front of all those people. That was irrational and childish. I told myself I'd go slow with you, but then I went and proposed to you instead. Of course, you would run from that. Any normal person would. I just…I just didn't want what we had to feel temporary to you. I wanted to show you that our relationship could be rock solid. I wanted you to be able to count on me, on us."

I sat there and just stared at him. New tears trickled down my face. In front of me was the type of man I'd never even dared to dream about. Although we came from completely different backgrounds, we both, in our own ways, needed to feel loved. I realized he was just as scared as I was, thinking this could crash and burn, but he was willing to give it a go if I was.

I reached across the cab of his truck and reclaimed his hand. "I'm sorry, too. I'm sorry I ran. It's what I do when I get scared." My voice was thick with emotion, but the hope that lit up in his eyes affirmed I had said the right thing. "I don't want to run anymore. I really *do* want to be with you, I'm just not very good at it. Clearly."

"That's okay. I'm a good teacher," he said softly.

As fresh snow began to cover the windshield, he leaned in for a kiss. His lips were soft at first and then slowly grew more passionate.

"You know," I panted, between kisses, "there was another reason I said no to your proposal."

He stopped kissing me and pulled back. "Oh? And why is that?"

I placed my hand on his thigh, really high up on his thigh. So high, I could feel his jeans shift in excitement, even in the cold.

"Well, it's just…how could I marry a man before I knew if we were, you know, sexually compatible?" I bit my lip as seductively as I could in the cold air.

He actually moaned. "Oh, well, maybe we can find that out sometime?"

"How about right now?" I asked.

His eyes danced for a moment at the open invitation. Scott checked around outside of the truck windows that had already fogged over from our breath.

"Right here. Right now." I clarified.

"Really? Are you sure? It's freezing in here. Your foot…"

"I'm not cold at all," I said, pulling my shirt over my head. "In fact. I'm pretty hot at the moment."

His eyes grew wide, landing firmly on the black bra I wore.

This was not like me. At all. I was never the one who initiated sex. I was the giver, not the taker. Yet, I couldn't deny that it felt wildly empowering. My body warmed at the strength of asking for what I wanted. I liked this new side of myself, and from the shock on Scott's face, so did he.

He reached across me and locked the passenger door. He patted my boot. "Don't want you falling out and getting hurt again."

I pulled him close to me, so his full weight was on me. "I'll be fine. And if I get hurt, you'll take care of me, right?"

He nodded. "I will."

And right there, in the middle of the driveway, in the middle of winter, in the middle of my life, I discovered that I was no longer merely a doppelganger of the strong, confident and successful girl I wanted to be. As of that moment, locked in his embrace, I had become the real deal.

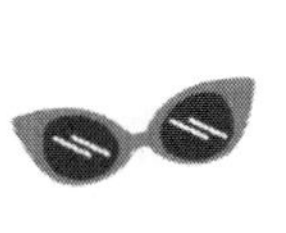

Epilogue

The knock on the door came far too early in the morning for any sane person to be up, so I instinctively knew it was Macy. I glanced at the clock and saw that it was almost seven. I smiled. Since moving in with Scott, I hadn't woken up at the crack of dawn anymore, as had been my norm. Lying in his arms until he pried me out of them was.

Not wanting to wake him up, I pulled back the covers carefully. He had gone to bed super late last night after cramming for his final. I smiled at the pile of medical books by his bedside table. After Morgan's money had come in, we decided to use it to pay for him to go back to school to be a Nurse Practitioner. I insisted he go, actually, as a condition of moving in with him. The hospital had a great demand for NPs, and he clearly wasn't living up to his full potential. He hedged a bit so to sweeten the deal, I told him I would marry him the day he got his degree. He signed up for classes that afternoon.

I didn't bother with a robe, opting to pull on Scott's flannel instead. I inhaled his scent as I wrapped it around my body.

It had been almost a year since I'd moved in and started my gig at the receptionist desk at the hospital where Scott worked. I saw him every day, and I still couldn't get enough of him. I found that I still needed constant reminders, like the scent of his clothes or seeing the toothbrush next to mine in the bathroom. It was so stupid, but they all reminded me this wasn't a dream. He really wasn't going anywhere.

I tiptoed across the room, silently cursing the creaky floorboards and gently turned the door handle in an attempt to sneak out of the bedroom.

"Tell Macy I said 'hi,'" Scott mumbled as he rolled over, opening one eye. "Sexy shirt, by the way."

Catching a glimpse of him in the ball of covers, I was annoyed that my efforts to keep quiet had failed but then quickly turned into mush when he gave me that sweet smile of his. Even half awake, his hair sticking up in all directions and his face covered with stubble, the man was delicious.

"I was trying not to wake you," I said, rushing back to the bed to sneak in a quick cuddle before I dealt with Macy. She could wait, my morning snuggle couldn't.

"I don't mind being woken up if I get to kiss you when I do," he said. He was still clearly exhausted, so I gave him one last peck and pushed him back down into the bed.

"Sleep. We can pick this up later."

"Mmm," he murmured playfully before he let me wrap the blankets around him again.

Tripod jumped off the bed too in hopes of getting an early breakfast. Her kittens were due any day. I hadn't told Scott yet that we were keeping them all. After all, it was his fault she got out and got knocked up in the first place.

I walked to the door and looked through the window to make sure it really was Macy and not some random person trying to sell me something or cut my head off. Her resulting frown confirmed that I'd taken far too long to answer the door. I held up an annoyed finger to tell her she'd have to wait a second.

After plopping a can of wet food down for a very fat Tripod, my eyes darted absently to Morgan's wedding invitation sitting on the counter, and I smiled. Her life had changed so much in such a short time. After getting her clean bill of health, Cassandra just assumed everything would return to normal, but it didn't. Gone were days of taking any and every role offered to her. Now, Morgan only did what challenged or inspired her, accepting parts she felt worthy of taking time away from the quiet life she'd made for herself in the mansion with Bernard.

Macy knocked lightly on the door again.

Blowing my hair out of my face I opened the door in a bit of a huff.

"You do realize it's seven o'clock in the morning, right?" I let out a thunderous yawn. "And before you start on me, I also know you're only here for the week, but couldn't we have caught up in a few hours?" I stepped out onto the porch and gestured to the patio chairs. "Scott's still asleep, or I'd invite you in."

I collapsed into the wicker chair ready to fall back to sleep myself, but a tiny pinch of a stray leaf on the chair kissed my exposed thigh, thwarting my attempt to drift off. A second later, I had to swat away a pesky black fly who believed I was his breakfast. I was still getting used to all of this nature stuff trying to eat me.

"The book went live today," Macy whispered, pulling her chair closer to me. Her voice was quiet. Shaky. She was nervous.

"Yes. I know. It's all you've talked about for days." She had a faraway look about her. "So…? How is it doing?"

She shook her head. “I don’t know. I’m too nervous to check. I mean the release party out in LA was great and all, but that doesn’t mean anything. People have ulterior motives at those things. It’s never about the book. Always about what is in it for them. Free publicity, making new contacts, rubbing elbows…that sort of shit.” She stood and paced on the porch. “Looking at the charts today is the real test to see if the book is doing well.”

“It’s a great book, Macy. I’m sure people are going to love it.”

“It’s all about timing. Authors get one small window to know if the last year of their life will amount to anything.”

This wasn’t the first time I’d had to talk Macy down before a book release, but it was definitely the most on edge she’d been. For good reason. The autobiography was the first book she had penned herself instead of as one of the firm’s celebrity ghostwriters. Morgan had insisted Macy’s name be on the cover as well, so this time, it was personal.

She’d spent months with Morgan, going over details, comparing notes, trying to get the most accurate description of her cushy life before the cancer, the desperation of the time in treatment and the eventual full and miraculous recovery. It really was a brilliant book…and just as much hers as

Morgan's. As a result of the upcoming tell-all book, Morgan's career was on fire again, and I was hoping, for Macy's sake, some of that luck would rub off on her.

"I needed to look at the list with you here…to help me work through the failure bullshit that will come if this thing has tanked," Macy said, stopping in front of me.

I nodded once and let out a breath. "Okay. Let's check," I replied, sighing and reaching for Macy's phone.

Macy reluctantly handed me the device. "I turned it off…didn't want to see anything until I got here."

She wiped her palms on her pants. I waited for her to signal she was ready, and then I put my hand on the power button. "One, two…" I didn't wait for three and turned the phone on. Macy closed her eyes and grimaced.

After her phone powered up, the notifications started to come in. One after another, like a chorus of chirping birds.

Macy risked opening one eye. "Well? Are those good dings, or bad dings?"

"Hang on, I'm still reading." I scanned the sea of notifications and pulled up an image sent to her from Cassandra.

"Oh, my God," I gasped.

"Oh, my God, what?" Macy's voice was on the verge of hysteria.

"It's sitting at number three, Macy."

Her other eye popped open.

"No shit?"

"No shit." I laughed.

She stole the phone from my hands and began to read the screen; her eyes grew wider when she saw her name on the New York Times Best Seller List.

A second later, she started jumping up and down and shouting at the top of her lungs.

"I did it. I did it! I finally did it!"

"Shhh! Macy, people, are still sleeping," I said, beaming at her. "Scott, being one of them."

"No, I'm not," his gruff morning voice said from behind me. He'd brought out three cups of coffee in a most precariously balanced way.

I quickly stood and grabbed two from him.

"I'm sorry we woke you, honey."

He kissed my head in that way that always made me feel unbelievably loved and cherished. "Don't be. What are we celebrating?"

I gave one of the cups to Macy, but she was too excited to drink it.

"Her book with Morgan dropped today. It's sitting at number three."

Scott let out a low whistle. "Well then, happy release day, Macy," Scott said, lacing his arm around me.

Macy thanked him and turned her attention back to her phone to call the office.

"You should be sleeping," I nagged.

Scott nuzzled my nose. "No. I should be right where I am."

He leaned in and gave me the most perfect early morning kiss anyone could ask for.

"Oh, my God," Macy squealed a moment later and bursting our blissful moment. "The publisher wants me to write another book!"

"That's wonderful," I said, taking a long sip of my coffee.

Macy's face contorted as she approached, placing her hand on my shoulder. "Oh, you don't understand." She grinned at me. The sort of grin she gave me only when she wanted something. "They want *your* story, Jules. They want the exclusive dish on your time as Morgan."

My eyes widened in shock. Even as I shook my head vehemently *no*, I knew she'd get me to agree.

I glanced up at Scott who was laughing.

"I think I'm gonna need a lot more coffee before I answer you." I sighed.

Scott smiled. "I know a good place. Let me take you all to breakfast. I hear they make a mean blueberry muffin."

My quiet little life was about to get interesting again.

Sneak Peek
Must Love Coffee

Chapter 1

MUST LOVE COFFEE. I frowned at the words on the screen. Those three words were the only ones I could think to list in my "wants" section of this stupid online dating site. For the last half hour, I'd been staring at the screen, trying to come up with something better. Apparently, having an addiction to caffeine was the only thing I wanted.

That wasn't totally true, but it's not like you can say, *I'm looking for someone with big tits and who's great in bed.* Women don't care for that. I had to be serious. I needed to list things that reflected who I was. What was I besides a coffee shop owner?

Therein was the problem. No chick in their right mind was going to love a balding, four-eyed guy in his mid-forties, who had no aspirations outside of waking up in the morning without a hangover.

Twenty years ago I could have bragged about my dreams of starting a band and traveling the world. But now, my guitar sat collecting dust in my perpetual bachelor pad. I was no longer the sort of guy a girl would be jumping up and down to meet, let alone date.

That's not to say I was this hideous creature from a horror movie. It's just, over the last ten years or so, I'd become…average—nothing to write home about. The sort of person you'd pass on the street and not even notice.

Somehow, I'd become an adult who couldn't even keep a house plant alive. A few years ago, that idea didn't faze me in the least. Staring down the barrel of middle age terrified me. I was going to die alone if something didn't change.

Hence the dating sites. I needed to branch out of my tiny town of Bucksville, New Hampshire. Because, as my sister, Jackie, had so eloquently put it: "You've slept with every woman in a ten-mile radius over the years. Online dating is your only option left."

That wasn't true. Well, not really. I hadn't slept with *all* the women in this town, just a dozen or so…several times over. That wasn't my fault, though. There weren't a lot of options in a small town.

Maybe that's what started this sudden mid-life panic. The old standby girls just weren't doing it for me anymore. I was craving…I don't know, something more.

"What's wrong with one-night stands, Finny, old boy?" my pal Joe had asked one night at the bar, wiggling his thick eyebrows. Joe had been my dad's best friend and was in the pub more often than in his day job, it seemed. His face was always red from drink, which stood out against a bad bleached-blond hair dye. It was a look that may have made him attractive back in the day, but now made his bloated face stand out like a stop sign.

I'd known Joe since I was a kid. After Dad passed, Joe sort of stepped in, thinking I needed a father figure. Or maybe he just wanted a drinking buddy. Dad had never been a big drinker, but I sure was after his death. Joe had seen some of my darkest days. He cleaned up my drunken messes more times than a friend should, I'm ashamed to admit.

"Finn, you're in the prime of your life," Joe had said the other night. "This is when you should be going out and buying a convertible, banging some college chick, or moving to Paris. It's not the time to settle down!"

Joe was talking out of his ass. He was happily married, and as far as I knew, as faithful as they came. Still, he was getting older and likely wanted to live vicariously through my bad life choices. And boy, oh boy, did I make a few of those.

"I gotta grow up sometime, Joe. I'm not in college anymore," I said, nursing the last of my beer.

College. Man, back then, there had been no shortage of women vying for a spot on my arm. All the sorority girls wanted to date the hunky grunge rocker who played free gigs at their parties. It didn't matter they didn't know my name or even what my major was. The truth was, I didn't care about theirs either.

After college I had plans—epic, backpacking through Europe plans—except, I didn't have the cash to do it. So, I'd decided I'd earn my way there by taking on a few shifts at my folks' shop, Must Love Coffee. A summer job. That turned into working just a few months after the season ended. Then, months turned into years, and all my grand aspirations of a better life outside of the snore-inducing Bucksville faded away, right along with my hairline.

Things were monotonous until Ma was killed by a drunk driver, and I went into a tailspin when Dad died of a heart attack three months later. From that point on, life pretty much sucked.

I was thirty-five when they passed. A full decade had slid through my fingers…and what had I done in that time? Other than keeping the shop open? Nothing. I hadn't even moved out of the stupid little apartment above the shop I'd had when I was in college. I had made no attempt to better my situation, so it was my own fault. And yet, I was still bitter with the universe that my life hadn't magically morphed into something meaningful all on its own.

"You just haven't found your purpose yet," Jackie had told me one morning over the phone.

"My purpose?" My eyes practically rolled out of my head.

"Yes. That thing, or person, who's going to make you want to be a better man."

I snorted. "You don't think I'm a good man now?"

Her voice dropped to a whisper. "I think you have the potential to be so much more than you are."

I wasn't convinced of the potential part, but I did feel like I was stuck in a rut. For the last ten years, I'd been on autopilot, surviving from day to day. I woke up, went to work, headed to the bar, and then back home. That was it.

There had to be more to life than that. Right? I found I was craving someone to come home to at the end of a day—someone to talk to, to hold, and grow old with. It was sappy, but it was the truth.

I suppose that's why I relented to my sister's endless suggestions of online dating. So far, however, no one was turning my eye in the surrounding towns.

I deliberately left out the area I lived in on my search because besides knowing everyone here, there wasn't anything exciting about Bucksville. We had a population of just over a thousand people. There was one grocery store and one fast food joint but three gas stations. Why we needed so many, I had no idea.

About the biggest excitement we had in Bucksville was that we had a movie star who vacationed here from time to time. She lived up in a big-ass mansion on Miller Street. The town went nuts when she bothered to show her face to the locals, but thankfully, that wasn't often. My staff still liked to talk about the day she had come into the shop for coffee. I definitely didn't want someone as high-maintenance as her. I wanted a woman who'd look hot in both heels and sweats and who'd steal a slice of pizza out of my hands. It wouldn't hurt if she loved hockey, either. Could I say that in the ad? Probably make me look like a jackass.

I shook my head at the waiting cursor on my computer screen and blew out a breath of defeat. This was getting nowhere. I closed my laptop and focused on the waiting pile of bills on my desk. I shouldn't really call it a desk. It's a card table tucked into the former walk-in pantry I'd converted into an office. It wasn't pretty, but it did the trick.

As I cut checks, I fought off a yawn. It was late. The shop had long since closed. I wanted to go home, have a beer, maybe watch some porn, and go to bed. That was the sucky part of being a shop owner. Bills had to be tended to regardless of what I wanted.

I spent several aggravating minutes shoving paid invoices into the overstuffed filing cabinet in the corner. I cursed myself for not going digital. One of these days, I'd take the time and do it, but I didn't have the patience to learn a new way when the old one worked just fine.

Christ, I'm starting to sound like my dad.

When I reached the bottom of the waiting envelopes, I noticed it wasn't another bill but rather a letter. The envelope only said "Finn" on the outside.

Tearing it open, I adjusted my glasses to read the small handprint, which looked like it was scribbled down in haste.

I recognized the writing as Kenny's. Kenny was my only full-time barista. He was the real reason the shop did so well. That man knew how to make a mean cup of coffee. Kenny trained all the other part-timers how to use the machines, but none of them were particularly good at it. I knew I should give him a raise, but the funds weren't there.

Curious about why he'd write me a letter versus talking to me in the morning, I tore it open and skimmed over his words. I clutched my stomach as it rolled over. It was his letter of resignation. He'd taken a better paying job at a shop the next town over. It was closer to his daughter's school and offered him medical coverage.

"Shit."

I couldn't counter that offer.

The letter was his two-week notice. I had fourteen days to find a barista willing to work full-time for a measly minimum wage job with no benefits.

Opening my laptop again, I went to our community bulletin board website to post a help-wanted ad. I began it with the line MUST LOVE COFFEE.

Find the series in ebook or paperback!

Acknowledgments

My sincere thanks to all of the early alpha readers of this book, the unlucky few who got to read the really ugly first drafts: my mom, Sharon Estes; Julie Cassar; and Kari Suderely. Their comments helped mold the story into what it is today. Also, many thanks are owed to my beta readers who read the second draft and found the bumps in the road I couldn't see. Those brave souls are Jenn Tenney, Jeanne McCartney, and Cassy Bunnell.

It is because of great readers like you that I put my butt in the chair each day and write. Thank you.

Also, a hearty thanks goes out to my editor, Kathy Lapeyre, who turned my manuscript blood red in order to make it shine.

Author Bio

Danielle Bannister a.k.a. Dani Bannister is a romance author who lives with her two children in Midcoast Maine along with her precious peppermint mocha creamer. She holds a BA in Theatre from the University of Southern Maine and her Masters in Literary Education from the University of Orono. When she's not on the stage, or on the page, you'll find her curled up with a good book. As one does.

You can visit her website at:
http://daniellebannister.com/
or
You can also join her newsletter at:
https://bookhip.com/BZHAHJM

Also by the Author

THE ROMANCES

The ABCs of Dee
Doppelganger
Must Love Coffee
Taking Stock
What Moons Do
The First 100 Kisses
The Second 100 Kisses
Where You Left Me-Vol. 1
Where You Left Me-Vol. 2
Where You Left Me-Vol. 3
Where You Left Me-Vol. 4
Where You Left Me-Vol. 5
Waiting in the Wings

FANTASY/PARANORMAL/SUSPENSE

The Hallowed Realms Trilogy with Amy Miles:
Netherworld, Hollow Earth, Isle of Glass
The Lurkers Within: A Havenwood Falls Novella
The Twin Flames Trilogy*:*
Pulled, Pulled Back, and *Pulled Back Again*
Girl on Fire

Made in the USA
Middletown, DE
03 August 2024

58163383R00208